Enthusiastic Praise for

Barbara Delinsky

"One of today's quintessential authors of contemporary fiction... Ms. Delinsky is a joy to read. With the incisive skill of a surgeon and the delicate insight of true compassion, she deeply probes the quality and meaning of life.... Women's fiction at its very finest."
—*Romantic Times*

"[An author] of sensitivity and style."
—*Publishers Weekly*

"Ms. Delinsky has a special knack for zeroing in on the pulse of her characters immediately—we know them and understand what makes them tick within the first few pages.... Well done!"
—*Rendezvous*

"When you care enough to read the very best, the name of Barbara Delinsky should come immediately to mind.... One of the few writers... who still writes a great love story, Ms. Delinsky is truly an author for all seasons."
—*Rave Reviews*

It wasn't enough—for him or for her

"Should I stop?" John murmured, pulling Pepper more fully into his embrace. His lips brushed her lightly, fueling their hunger.

"Oh, no, this feels so good." Her eyes were alight, her lips parted in the faintest smile of fascination. Encouraged, he slipped his fingers beneath her bodice and tugged gently at the gauzy material.

Pepper didn't demur, even when her breasts were bared to his gaze. Her nipples puckered in response, and when he touched one, a shock of energy sizzled through her body....

"Oh, Pepper!" John whispered hoarsely. "You're magnificent."

Barbara DELINSKY

JASMINE SORCERY

Harlequin Books

TORONTO • NEW YORK • LONDON
AMSTERDAM • PARIS • SYDNEY • HAMBURG
STOCKHOLM • ATHENS • TOKYO • MILAN
MADRID • WARSAW • BUDAPEST • AUCKLAND

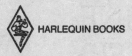 HARLEQUIN BOOKS

JASMINE SORCERY
© 1986 by Barbara Delinsky

ISBN 0-373-83248-6

First Harlequin Books printing September 1986

Reprinted August 1992

Printed in U.S.A.

1

PEPPER MACNEIL pulled the key from the ignition of her Rabbit and twisted in her seat to gather the pile of letters and magazines. Casey Lane, the quiet country way where she was parked, was her favorite stretch of her mail delivery route, for she walked it rather than simply driving from one rural box to the next. Here there were people—warm people, friendly people. She was looking forward to seeing them again.

Sliding from her seat, she paused to savor the richness of summer in Maine. She'd been gone for only two weeks, yet the trees looked more lush, the flowers more colorful. Perhaps it was an appreciation of home, she mused. As exciting as Europe had been, as beautiful the cities she'd visited, she was glad to be back.

Balancing the bundle of mail on her hip, she headed for the first house. A simple frame structure of Victorian design, it was painted white, as was the crisp picket fence around its lawn. A huge maple shaded her path from the strong morning sun. A mock orange bush, its white blossoms filling the air with perfume, awaited her.

She moved lithely along the paved walk, easily taking the four wooden steps leading up to the veranda. When she had nearly reached the door it opened, and a small, gray-haired woman emerged, smiling broadly.

"Pepper! It's so good to see you! How was your trip?"

Pepper grinned. "Wonderful, Mrs. Burns. Absolutely wonderful." Lifting several letters from the top of her pile, she held them out. "Vienna was magnificent, just as you said it would be."

"Mind you, I've never been there," the older woman cautioned, "but my daughter's been raving about it for years. Y'heard your music?"

"Oh, yes. You can't imagine what a thrill it was ... to be there where so much of it was written, then to hear it played in the most charming garden settings you've ever seen." She blinked and sighed. "Yes, I heard my music."

"Mozart?"

"Mozart *and* Strauss *and* Schubert. Waltzes drifting over treetops, dinners serenaded by violins, Danube park ... it was wonderful!"

"Must be hard to come back."

"Oh, no. It's great. I missed you all."

The woman hugged the letters to her chest in lieu of Pepper herself. "Well, we missed you, too."

Pepper treasured the warmth in her words. In the ten short months that she'd been the U.S. Postal Services rural carrier for the town of Naples, she'd found an acceptance she'd never known before.

"How are you feeling? Is the arthritis behaving itself?"

Mrs. Burns smiled sheepishly. "As much as y'can expect, given that I'm an old lady."

"You're not an old lady."

The other held up a gnarled hand. "Uh, uh, let's not start all this again. Nothin' you can say, Pepper Mac-

Neil, can take any of these seventy-one years and make 'em go away. But I do love ya for your good intent." She paused, her eyes taking on an expectant gleam. Her voice lowered. "Have you seen 'im?"

Pepper raised her brows. "Seen him?"

"Him." The older woman cocked her head. "Down the street."

This time Pepper's brows furrowed. "Old Sam?"

"No, no, child. Not Old Sam. Old Sam's as pesky as those mosquitoes he's always cursin'. I'm talkin' about ... *him*."

Pepper's lips quirked in amusement. "No, I haven't seen *him*. Who is he?"

Mrs. Burns eyed her speculatively, then straightened and inched back into her house. "New neighbor. You'll see." She gestured with her hand. "Go. Go."

"Mrs. Burns...."

"Go, child. Move. I've got other things to do with my day than to stand jabberin' with the mailman." The screen door bounced shut as the older woman hobbled down the long front hall of her house.

Pepper stared after her for a minute before shaking her head, turning and retracing her steps. New neighbor? She dropped her gaze to the mail in her arms and was about to sift through for an unfamiliar name when, with a cacophony of happy yips, a blur of gold caught her attention. The new neighbor was forgotten.

"Rochester! You little scamp!" Grinning, she squatted to scratch the ears of the frisky cocker spaniel at her feet. But the puppy wouldn't stay still long enough. Its paws danced wildly, its nose darted time and again toward the pocket of her government issue Bermuda shorts. "Smart cookie, aren't you," she said, laughing as she tugged a doggie biscuit from the pocket under attack and held it up. The dog sat instantly, the only thing threatening its pose being its tail, which wouldn't quit.

"There you go." She released the biscuit just in time; it was never to be seen again. Only then was she able to scratch the silky fur between the puppy's long ears. "So you missed me, too, did you? I could swear you've grown a foot. Can't be calling you a puppy much longer—"

"Pepper!"

Pepper looked up to see a young woman approaching, the baby on her hip clinging to her long brown hair. "Sally! Hi!"

"Hi, yourself! I see you've been welcomed back properly. Nothing like a freeloader to tell you you've been missed."

Straightening, Pepper shrugged. "He's adorable." She put out a finger to the eight-month-old child, who quickly released her mother's hair in favor of a fresh attraction. "Not as adorable as this little one, though." Her tone softened appropriately. "How are you, Chrissie? You're looking very pretty today in your pink sunsuit." Chrissie was unimpressed by the compliment.

"A gift from my mother-in-law," Sally Brannigan explained. "She's convinced we don't have any stores in this neck of the woods. And nothing but Saks will do for her granddaughter. Of course, Saks might not care for the dirt that'll be on this little scrap of terry by the time the day's through."

"Dirt? She's crawling!"

Sally grinned. "Finally. I'd put her down and show you, but I'm driving over to Auburn in a little while and I don't want to have to bathe her again."

Side by side, the two women began to walk. Rochester gamboled in haphazard accompaniment. "Going shopping?"

Sally shook her head and looked at her daughter. "Meeting daddy for an early lunch. He had to take care of some business this morning, then he'll be heading north for a couple of days."

"Another sales trip." Pepper kept her tone sympathetic. Much as it angered her that Sally and Chrissie were left alone for days at a stretch, she knew her feelings on the score were far from impartial.

"Another sales trip. Easy this time, though. He should be back by Wednesday. Hey, you look wonderful. How was your trip?"

"Great. Really great." Freeing her finger from Chrissie's grasp, she reached for the Brannigans' mail and tucked it into the large front pocket of Sally's sundress.

"Thanks. The plane ride and everything was okay?"

"Smooth flying all the way."

"And the concerts?"

"Fantastic. You wouldn't have believed Salzburg, Sally. It was so quaint and beautiful. There were lectures. We toured Mozart's birthplace, his home, the Mozarteum.

I took scads of pictures. I'll bring them along as soon as they're developed."

They reached the Brannigans' front walk and stopped. "Have time for a cold drink? It's going to be a warm day."

"Thanks, Sal, but I'll take a rain check. Since I've been gone for two weeks, it would behoove me—" she drew out the word in comical fashion "—to move right along. Besides, you're going out."

"Not for another little while," Sally argued, then paused. "Have you . . . have you seen him?"

Pepper abruptly raised her eyes from Rochester's antics. "Him?"

"Mmmm. The new guy."

"Mrs. Burns just mentioned him. No, I haven't—"

"Wait'll you do. Some neighbor."

Pepper turned to her mail again and began to sort through in search of a name. Sally put a hand on her wrist. "Just wait. He'll make your day."

"I'm not sure I like that gleam in your eye, Sally Brannigan." Pepper's lips turned down. "Mrs. Burns wore one just like it. I didn't know anyone was moving. Who *is* this guy?"

"No one moved. He bought the Fletcher place."

"The Fletcher place?"

"You know, the mausoleum that's been empty all these months?"

"Ah." Pepper instantly conjured the image of a decrepit old man frightful enough to go with the house that was situated at the very end of the dead-end street. "The

Fletcher place. My Lord, it's been for sale since I moved here. What would anyone want with it?"

"Word has it he's planning to do it over."

The image in her mind changed to one of a robust gentleman wearing golf slacks stuffed with money. "He's a millionaire buying a summer home? It'll take bundles to get that thing in shape."

Sally looked smug. "Word has it he's planning to do it over himself."

"Himself?" The image altered again, this time to one of a brawny carpenter. "Oh, no. Machismo. Tell me the guy's got inflated biceps."

"Now, now, Pepper. I'm a married woman. Would I be looking at things like that?"

"You had to be looking at *something* to have that satisfied smirk on your face." She made a face of her own. "Maybe I'll take that cold drink, after all."

But Sally started up her front walk. "Sorry. Too late. Besides, you've got to be moving on. First day back from vacation and all." Pepper was sure she was grinning, but she didn't turn again.

"Chrissie," Pepper called, "you'd better watch out for that mother of yours. She's not being very nice."

As though at eight months the child understood just what was happening, she gave Pepper a wide, three-toothed grin over her mother's shoulder.

"Sally...?" She tried a final time.

"See you tomorrow, Pep. Have a good day." The smile in her voice persisted. Pepper suspected it even erupted into a chuckle as the second screen door of the day banged shut on her.

"Have a good day, yourself," Pepper told the air, then twirled on her heel and resumed her route. "Typical Maine," she mumbled, "all excited about a new face."

She wasn't being critical. The ways of the quiet townsfolk in Naples had intrigued her from the start. Yes, there was a certain wariness toward newcomers, particularly those transients who came to vacation, then left. Pepper herself was experiencing the seasonal influx for the first time. She'd started work right after Labor Day the fall before and so had missed the height of the season. Come June, the vacationers had begun to arrive, though. And now that it was July, her route would take several extra hours to complete each day.

She wondered how the summer people took to the locals. In her case she'd discovered that once the locals' wariness receded, there was a bounty of goodness remaining. She liked these people. They liked her. She was very comfortable in Naples. It occurred to her that she might stick around for a while.

It was a longer walk to the third house on the street. She breathed in the fragrant summer air, the smell of newly mown grass that never failed to strike a distant chord within her. She was always amazed when it happened, this sense of déjà vu. After all, she spent less than three years of her life in a town such as this, and she'd been so little then. That this particular smell should be familiar when she could remember nothing else of her time in Maine was remarkable. Then again, perhaps it wasn't, given all that had happened since she'd left.

Turning up the next walk, she drew herself from her reverie as Old Sam Thistle straightened from work on his petunia bed.

"If it isn't the wanderer," he stated with typically dry wit.

"Traveler, Sam. And it's good to be back."

"Good trip?"

"Ay-yup."

He twisted his mouth at her attempt to talk native. "Needs some work. Must'a forgot all I taught you while you were off galavantin' round the world."

Pepper smiled. "I see your good humor's intact. How've you been, Sam?" She handed him his mail, which he proceeded to examine with the same scowl.

"Not bad. Hmph. Bills. If it isn't the heat, it's the phone. Not that I call much of anywhere now'days. Friends're dyin' off one by one. Like flies." As though to make his point, he slapped his arm, then drew his hand back to study what he'd caught. "Damned 'skeetas. Get 'em every time. Stupid as hell."

With a chuckle, Pepper turned to leave. At Old Sam's next muttered words, though, she came to a halt.

"Seen 'im yet?"

She turned slowly. "No. Not yet."

Tossing his mail on the porch, Sam returned to his petunias. When he didn't speak, she prodded. "*He* must be quite something. You're the third person who's mentioned him."

"Good-lookin' guy."

The image began to expand. Bedroom eyes and a Hollywood smile. She wondered what more she would discover before she finally reached his house.

"Is he . . . nice?"

"Dunno."

"When did he move in?"

"Week before last."

She was about to ask his name when she reminded herself that she did, indeed, have that information at her fingertips. She had begun to walk on again, thumbing through the mail, when Sam's parting shot hit her.

"Careful, girl."

She turned. "Hmm?"

But the old man with the straw hat, the misbuttoned shirt and the pants that bagged beneath his bulging middle simply shooed her away with a wave of his hand. At least he hadn't swatted her with that tart tongue of his as he'd done on any number of other occasions, she mused. Even now she recalled past tidbits. "What's a pretty thing like you doin' carryin' mail?" "Married? Well, why in the hell not?" "Watch out for that Newell fellow. He's itchin' to get his hands on. . . ."

But there'd been no aggression this time. In fact, Old Sam had been unusually tame. Perhaps he was glad to see her back. That had to be it, she decided with a fond smile.

Shifting the mail on her hip, she headed toward the small house owned by the Thompson sisters. Spinsters, they were, and utterly charming. As always, they were seated on the veranda, each in her respective rocking chair. As always, Miss Millie was crocheting. As always, Miss Sylvie was reading the morning paper. Pepper wasn't quite sure when they'd come to be known as *Miss* Millie and *Miss* Sylvie, since they'd been raised right here, far from the Southern mansion the form of address would suggest. But Miss Millie and Miss Sylvie they remained; it was, indeed, part of their charm.

Both looked up at her approach. Both quickly put down their respective work and sat forward.

"Pepper MacNeil, welcome home!" Miss Millie bubbled.

Miss Sylvie echoed her enthusiasm. "It's good to see you, Pepper. Looks like traveling suits you. You're bright and perky—"

"She's always bright and perky," Miss Millie scolded, casting her sister a pointed frown. The frown was gone by the time her gaze returned to Pepper. "But you do look good. And that's a fine thing."

"Particularly," Miss Sylvie said, emphasizing each syllable, "since you'll be meeting the new neighbor in a bit. You haven't seen him yet, have you?"

Miss Millie's annoyance returned. "Of course she hasn't seen him. She just got back and she hasn't reached his house. How could she possibly have seen him yet?"

Miss Sylvie regarded her sister with disdain. "It's very possible, Millie, that she saw him around town this weekend." Her attention returned to Pepper. "You did get back Friday, didn't you?"

"Saturday—" Pepper began, only to be interrupted.

"You see, sister," Miss Millie scolded, "she hasn't had enough time to be wandering around town ogling every new face on the street. The dear Lord knows that this time of year there are plenty of those. And since this is her first day back on the job—"

"*I* know that," Miss Sylvie retorted, her chin tipped higher. "But he's no ordinary vacationer. And you know that just about everyone in town's been talking about him."

"Sounds pleasant," Pepper murmured, listening to the sisters' banter with an indulgence that was beginning to fray. Her first impulse was to drop her mail and run straightaway to the house at the far end of the street if for no other reason than to get a look at the man who'd set the town astir. Her second impulse, however, was the one she followed.

Very calmly gathering the Thompsons' mail from the top of the pile and extracting the latest issue of *Reader's Digest* and *Yankee* magazine from the bottom, she filled Miss Sylvie's waiting hands.

"Now, why ever do they do that?" Miss Sylvie exclaimed, exasperated at sight of the magazines. "I've written to them more than once. Send them on different days, I say. Stagger your mailings. I can only read one thing at a time. But, no. They insist on issuing them si-mul-taneously."

"Sylvie," Miss Millie said, sighing wearily, as though they'd had the same discussion many times, "those magazines are put out by different publishers."

"I know that. But it's no excuse. They've got to be aware of each other's publication schedules. They ought to be more attentive to their readers."

Miss Millie spoke as though to an infant. "Put one of the magazines away in the back room, Sylvie. Then you can surprise yourself with it when you're done reading the first."

With a gentle smile, Pepper turned. "I'll leave you ladies to work out the details of whatever plan you decide on. See you tomorrow."

As though suddenly remembering Pepper's presence, Miss Sylvie looked up. "Now, Pepper, you talk with him. You hear?"

Pepper paused. "Talk with him?"

"That's right." For once, Miss Millie was in agreement with her sister. "Don't just walk up and deposit the mail in his slot." She frowned and looked away. "Does he have a slot? Or is it a box? Or is it. . . ." With urgency, her eyes sought Pepper's again. "If he's put up a thing at the end of the drive, ignore it. *Hand* him his mail. Tell him you're just wanting to welcome him to town. Give him one of those beautiful smiles of yours. Do it, Pepper!"

The smile Pepper showered on the ladies was not one of those beautiful ones. Rather, it was slightly forced and disappeared the instant she turned and began walking again. "He'll get his mail," she stated. "One way or another."

First, though, Pepper delivered mail to the Shaws, neither of whom were home, then to the Biddles, one of whom was.

"Good to see you, dear," Mrs. Biddle said, coming to the front door the instant she heard Pepper's footfall on the step. "And how was your vacation?"

"Just wonderful. Not terribly restful what with traveling from city to city, but it was well worth every minute."

"I'm glad. But we missed you. You're always prompt. It's so nice to get the mail in the morning."

Pepper smiled. Ever the diplomat, Mrs. Biddle wouldn't utter a direct complaint. During rainy spells, she'd wistfully eye the sky and talk of how beautiful the sun would make everything look. If the plumber didn't show up, she raved about the electrician who did. When her sister-in-law from Rhode Island was visiting, she extolled the virtues of solitude.

"You have to forgive Will," Pepper offered. "He must have been bogged down with the summer swell. It wasn't the best time for me to go away, though I had no choice if I wanted to be on that tour." Handing the woman her mail, Pepper held her breath, wondering how long it would take Mrs. Biddle to mention her new next-door neighbor. For the Fletcher house was indeed next door. Granted, it was out of sight, separated from the Biddles by half an acre of forested land. But it was the next stop on Pepper's route. And it was, in fact, the next thing on Mrs. Biddle's mind.

"Have you seen him yet?" the woman asked, arching one brow toward the brown hair that was pulled back into a neat bun.

"Not yet," Pepper replied, feeling as though she were a broken record.

Mrs. Biddle's second brow rose to mirror its mate. "Goin' there next?"

"Uh-huh."

"I can remember my Paul at his age." She sighed. "A good-looking devil if you ever saw one."

Pepper had met Mrs. Biddle's mild-mannered husband on an occasional Saturday and, though he was thoroughly pleasant, she seriously doubted that he'd ever been a devil, much less good-looking. She wondered if Mrs. Biddle was making an indirect statement about her new neighbor, and was about to make some subtle inquiry when the woman went on. "Men should be married by the time they're thirty. Should have a slew of children running around the yard. 'Specially up here." She tossed her head toward the forested half-acre. "Perfect place to raise children." A wrinkle marred her otherwise smooth brow. "Least ways, that was what I thought. Of course, the kids had other ideas. All three of them are in the city now. Two in Boston, one in Pittsburgh."

With a wave, Pepper turned. "I believe you got a letter from Pittsburgh today." She trotted down the steps. She'd heard all about the Biddle offspring and didn't have time to hear more today. For one thing, there was half an armload of mail yet to be delivered, not to mention the piles left in the car. For another, there was . . . him.

Pepper barely heard Mrs. Biddle's, "Thank you, dear. Have a nice day." Curiosity sparked her step as she turned right onto the sidewalk and headed for the Fletcher place. Was he married? She wasn't sure exactly how to interpret Mrs. Biddle's chatter, but half suspected that the new neighbor neither was married nor had a slew of children running around the yard.

Glancing down, she studied the next piece of mail in her pile. Even had she not been so thoroughly alerted, she would have learned about the new resident when she found his mail sandwiched between the Biddles' and the Carsons', the latter of whom lived directly across the street and on the return side of her route.

Walking steadily, she thumbed through the mail and found four pieces for *him*. The first three were official-looking envelopes; the fourth caught her eye. Sliding it to the top of the pile, she ran her fingertips over the fine ivory vellum. Though there was no return address in the upper left-hand corner, it was very obviously from a woman.

Coming to a halt beneath a broad birch, she glanced at the letter, then sniffed. Not freshly mown grass. Or mock orange blossoms. Or ever-present spruce. Slowly she raised the envelope to her nose.

"Lavender."

Scents were her specialty. She tried to recall everything she knew about lavender. In aromatherapy it was used to tone muscles and relieve aches. In the sixteenth and seventeenth centuries in England, where lavender thrived, it had been thought to give "comfort to the brain," to "pierce the senses" in a refreshing manner. Even earlier, it had been used by the Romans for its ability to absorb heat.

Pepper could believe the last. The letter in her hand seemed suddenly hot. She quickly dropped it atop the pile, then stared at it. The stamp read Love, the postmark New York. And the address had been written in a broad, flowery, red-inked script.

John Smith.

Pepper made a face and, mildly incredulous, studied the name again. Naples's new resident, the man about whom every neighbor on the street seemed to be talking, the recipient of a lavishly lavender love letter was named John Smith?

She laughed and shook her head, then began to walk again. John Smith. As ordinary a name as could be. And despite the excitement his arrival had seemed to generate, he was to her no more than another stop on her route.

Turning in at the pebbled drive, she eyed the tall firs that bordered it before yielding to a broad lawn broken by aged maples. The last time she'd been there it was to turn her Rabbit around in the rain. Then, the grass had grown wild; now it was freshly mowed. Her gaze skipped ahead to the house. It was a large Georgian colonial whose columns were peeling, whose windows were broken in places, whose shutters hung at odd angles. Though the brickwork on the front facade was intact, if mellow looking, the paint on the sides had seen far better days.

Yes, it was every bit as run-down a monstrosity as she'd remembered it . . . with one difference. High on its roof, applying new shingles, was a man.

John Smith.

Pepper stopped in her tracks and stared. For an instant she recalled the various images she'd conjured of him. The man high above, as yet oblivious to her presence, was no decrepit old patriot to match his home. Nor did he look like a millionaire, pockets stuffed with money. His denim cutoffs did have pockets, but they were molded so comfortably to his lean hips that she doubted anything was in them.

The cutoffs were all he wore. Swallowing once, she continued her analysis.

Biceps? Not overly inflated, though his back was broad and the arms that worked at holding and hammering shingles looked strong. The play of muscles beneath his skin was concise; he seemed hard, lean, well toned.

With a shaky breath, Pepper inadvertently inhaled the lavender scent that suddenly seemed oppressively heavy. If John Smith was a playboy from New York, he had a strange way of showing it. Even from the distance, she saw that his skin, tanned but with the hint of a fresh burn, glistened with sweat. His sandy-gray hair was thick and long enough to graze his neck. His legs were well formed, firm and leanly sinewed. His bare feet braced his body on the roof with ease.

Pepper shivered, the tiny movement jolting her from her thoughts. She was the mail carrier, for heaven's sake. She was paid to deliver the mail, not to stand in driveways and stare at strange men on roofs.

Launching into a confident gait, she approached the house.

"Hello!" she called out in her most assured tone, shielding her eyes to look up as the angle sharpened.

John Smith turned his head then, and Pepper found herself staring once more. The sandy-gray hair that had grazed his neck also hung low on his brow. The shadow of a beard covered his square jaw. His face gleamed with sweat as his back had done, and the light swirls of hair on his chest looked damp.

If Pepper was staring, John Smith was doing no less. He took in the richness of her thick sable hair, drawn back from her cheeks and brow into a French braid at her crown, a braid that then blended with the heavy fall draped behind her shoulders. Her face was the palest shade of gold, her features strong, yet delicate in a purely feminine sort of way. He doubted she wore any makeup, for the faint flush on her cheeks and lips looked natural and exquisitely healthy. Though the pale blue-gray shirt she wore was masculine in style, as were her darker Bermuda shorts, neither could hide the soft swell of her breasts, the narrowness of her waist, the subtle flair of her hips.

He blinked, then mopped his sweaty brow with his forearm. Was it a uniform she was wearing? And in her arms . . . ?

A vague sense of disbelief cast his features into puzzlement. "You're the mailman...mailwoman...uh, mailperson?"

His uncertainty, instantly endearing, restored to Pepper the confidence she'd momentarily lost. She grinned. "Any of the three. Take your pick." To her surprise, John Smith turned onto his backside and began to ease himself down to the ladder propped against the roof's edge. "Don't come down," she interjected. "I just wanted to say 'hi.' I can leave the mail—"

But he was already descending the ladder, the sinews of his calves and thighs tightening on each rung. Pepper moved back and lowered her eyes. Sally had been right. John Smith was "some neighbor." Pepper had to admit that he added something to the neighborhood.

On the ground at last, he turned and held out his hand. "John Smith. And you are...?"

He was very tall. Even barefooted, he towered over her by eight inches at least. She met his handclasp to find it warm and strong.

"Pepper MacNeil, mail carrier, at your service."

"Pepper MacNeil." He repeated the name and decided that it matched both the light freckles on her nose and the pixielike smile she wore. "And you do work for the postal service?"

She thrust out her left breast, with the official badge emblazoned on its pocket. Then, realizing what she'd done, she blushed and quickly changed the subject. "So you've actually bought this place?"

"Uh-huh. I've never met a lady mailman before."

"I'm not unique. You're going to fix it up yourself?"

"I'm going to try. Were you hired just for the summer?"

She shook her head. "I'm the regular carrier. I've been on vacation for the past two weeks, which is why you haven't seen me before. It's quite an undertaking, renovating this old house."

He cast a quick glance behind. "So I'm discovering. How long have you been carrying?"

Pepper's laugh was light as an evening breeze in the far willow. "You make it sound like a disease."

"No, no, I didn't mean that," he answered with such genuine concern that she instantly relented.

"Ten months. I started last fall."

"You enjoy it?"

She made a visual sweep of the landscape and breathed in deeply. "On a day like this, who wouldn't?" Her gaze landed on the roof. "You're making the most of the weather, I see."

He followed her gaze, but only for a moment. He'd rather look at Pepper MacNeil than slate shingles any day. Her eyes were a nondescript hazel shade, yet seemed to sparkle in a way that wasn't nondescript at all.

"I figure I'd better get the roof done first so anything else I do won't get ruined when it rains. It does rain up here, doesn't it?"

Pepper raised her brows. "Oh, yes. A mail carrier doesn't forget *those* days."

"Get pretty wet?"

"Pretty."

"You are."

"Excuse me?"

"You are. Pretty, that is." He was looking at her nose, which was short and slightly turned up at the tip, and he wondered how old she was. She didn't look more than twenty-two. When she proceeded to blush, he amended that to twenty.

"Thank you," she said softly, wondering why she suddenly felt shy. Unfortunately, her tongue didn't share the affliction. "So are you. Handsome, that is. They warned me. I should have been prepared."

To Pepper's astonishment, it was John's turn to blush, which he did in a way that was both boyish and manly and utterly charming. There was something about him, she decided, that was decidedly appealing. Then he smiled, and things went from bad to worse. For his smile was not like any she'd ever seen. Oh, she'd seen even white teeth before, but . . . the corners of his lips turned down.

"Remarkable," she murmured, not realizing she'd spoken aloud until John picked her up on it.

"What is?"

"Your smile. It's . . . it's—"

"Upside down? So I've been told."

"But you are smiling. . . ."

"Oh, yes. I don't think I've met anyone as fresh as you—"

Eyes widening, Pepper interrupted. "I'm sorry. I didn't mean to be fresh. . . ."

Again that smile, this time even broader. "Not fresh as in offensive. Fresh as in bright and uninhibited. You're delightful."

Barely recovering from the second smile, Pepper forced herself to wince. "I think this conversation's going nowhere. And I'm keeping you from your work."

"I needed to take a break anyway."

"Well, then, *I've* got work to do. If the mail can get through come rain, sleet or snow, it sure better get through in the bright sunshine."

"You won't stop for a cold drink?"

Her mouth was dry, her skin superwarm. But she didn't dare. "Uh, no, I don't think I'd better. I really have to run. Just wanted to welcome you to Naples." Wouldn't Miss Millie be pleased?

Pepper turned and began to walk, but the movement stirred the air enough to bring a floral scent to her nose. Lavender. She stopped abruptly and dropped her gaze to the mail hooked into her elbow.

"Oh, dear," she mumbled, grasping John Smith's four letters as she turned back to him. His smile was knowing, almost challenging. She thrust the letters toward him. "Nice one on top there. A little heavy on the scent. She must have worried it'd fade in transit. Determined lady."

And with that, Pepper turned smoothly and retraced her steps down the drive.

John stared after her until she'd rounded the evergreen grove and disappeared from sight. Even longer he stood there, wondering how such a beautiful day could have been improved upon. But it had. Pepper MacNeil, mailperson, had added spice.

Almost inadvertently he glanced down at the letters in his hand. From the topmost one came the scent Pepper had mentioned. She was right—it was heavy. Pepper, on the other hand, had a scent of her own. It was faint, coming only to him in wisps, as when she'd reached out to shake his hand and then again when she'd turned to leave. It was light, so light. Alluring as it was elusive.

He shook his head to free himself of the memory. She was young, too young. Hell, she wasn't much older than the students he counseled! *Wise up, old man. Act your age.* With a sigh, he glanced down at Monica's elaborate script. Then, slipping her letter to the back of the pile, he tossed the letters onto a rotting step and returned to the roof.

Farther down the street, Pepper made her remaining deliveries. She chatted with various neighbors who were home, telling them of her trip, asking what had happened in their lives while she'd been gone. When the inevitable question came—"Have you seen him?"—she simply nodded and smiled and commented on what a nice fellow he appeared to be.

Settling back into her car, she smiled to herself. He was a nice fellow. Intimidating at first with his good looks and superior height, but very down to earth. Almost . . . shy? No, gentle. Relaxing. Easy to talk to.

She wondered what he would do here in Naples, once he fixed up that white elephant of his, and knew that she could count on town gossip to eventually fill her in. She wondered where he'd come from, and half wished she'd paid as much attention to those other three letters of his as she'd paid to the lavender one.

Turning the key in the ignition, she pulled into Mrs. Burns's driveway to turn around. He had nice eyes, too, she mused. Pale gray, matching the streaks in his sandy hair. Nice looking fellow, indeed.

Then Old Sam's parting crack came back to her. "Careful, girl," he had said, and suddenly she knew what he'd meant.

2

TUESDAY MORNING DAWNED as clear and bright as Monday had been. Pepper picked up her mail, loaded the Rabbit and set out. As she drove, she hummed the theme of the Rachmaninoff rhapsody she'd listened to the night before.

She felt good. Rested and relaxed. Much of it, she knew, had to do with the long, scented bath she'd taken at dawn. Jasmine had a way with her; of all the florals, she responded most positively to it.

As always, she remained in her car for the first hour of deliveries, depositing mail in the rural boxes perched at the end of long lanes or driveways, stopping to talk with the occasional neighbor out walking. Her spirits were higher than ever when she parked at the corner of Casey Lane and hefted her load.

Mrs. Burns was there to greet her.

"Mornin', Pepper. Fine one, isn't it?"

"Indeed, Mrs. Burns."

"Well?"

"Yes?"

"What did you think?"

"About . . . ?"

"Him."

"Oh. Nice man."

The old woman smiled. "Good."

Sally Brannigan's thoughts ran along a similar vein. "Did you see him?" she was quick to ask, as soon as she'd given Pepper a rundown on lunch the day before.

Chrissie started to fuss, and Pepper turned her attention to the child, stroking fine gold-white hairs away from the little girl's face. "What's wrong, sweetie?"

"She's teething. Or missing Chris. Or something else, who knows. If only she could talk. Come on, Pepper. Did you see him?"

"I saw him."

"And . . . ?"

Pepper grinned innocently. "And what, Sal?"

"Wasn't he something?"

It amused Pepper that one John Smith could cause such a stir. He was only a man, she told Sally.

"But *quite* a man," Sally countered. "He was down here the other night talking with Chris about the best place to get lumber. He was so pleasant. So friendly. Chrissie was climbing all over him by the time he left."

"Chrissie wasn't asleep?"

Sally shrugged. "With Chris gone so often, I let her spend as much time as she can with him. But you're changing the subject. Is he gorgeous or is he gorgeous?"

"Not bad," was all Pepper would say before she gave Chrissie a kiss and took her leave.

Old Sam was even more direct. "Didn't make a pass at you, did he?"

"A pass? Sam, I'm the *mailman*."

Sam snorted from behind his trellis. The roses were in bloom, and beautiful. The loving care he gave them more than compensated for his oft-fractious way with people. "You're a *woman*, girl," he scoffed, oblivious of his contradictory choice of words.

Pepper took them in good spirit. "And you're a sweet man with a wonderful green thumb." She reached up to touch a velvety red petal. "These are beautiful. How do you get them to climb so high?"

"Love, girl. Love. They got thorns, though. Take care."

If there was a deeper message he offered, Pepper decided that the advice was unnecessary. She was immune to love, made so by a tragic case of it when she was a child. Since then she'd steered clear, and she would continue to do so. Indeed she remembered Sam's warning of yesterday and she had every intention of taking care. John Smith was handsome, and he seemed to like her. She was determined to keep that "like" on a plane she could handle.

The sisters Thompson were waiting, Miss Millie crocheting, Miss Sylvie reading the paper, each in her respective rocker. On more than one occasion Pepper had wondered if a name was etched somewhere on each chair lest one be accidentally swapped with the other. Today, though, she had no time for such musings.

"Good morning, Pepper," Miss Millie said.

"How are you today?" Miss Sylvie chimed in.

"She's just fine, sister," Miss Millie answered. Quite used to being talked about by the two, Pepper simply listened with a smile on her face. "Look at her. Glowing, I'd say."

"She's always glowing. It's part of her per-son-al-ity."

"I know that, Sylvie. But she looks even more glowing today." Millie lowered her voice. "Do you suppose she's dressing up for *him?*"

Pepper winced. "Dressing up? This is my uniform!"

She might as well have saved her breath. Miss Sylvie picked up right where her sister had left off. "Maybe. Her cheeks are pinker, now that I think about it."

Miss Millie began to crochet. "He looks like a loner to me. Drives in and out of here in that shiny new thing of his and the passenger side's always empty."

Pepper recalled the lavender letter and kept her mouth shut. Mildly surprised without knowing quite why, she added a flashy sports car to the image of John Smith, then waited, curious to hear what else the Thompsons had to say.

Miss Sylvie didn't disappoint her. "Not married. That much we know. Said something to Ed Walsh—he's the realtor who sold him the house—about being divorced. Don't know how recent it was, though."

Couldn't be too recent, Pepper mused, still thinking of the letter he'd received the day before. Of course, it might have been from his ex-wife, or an "other" woman. Maybe John Smith had betrayed his wife and thereby destroyed the marriage. But then why would he be here, while the lavender lady was in New York? Maybe she planned to join him after the house was in suitable shape for a woman of her obviously lavish taste. Strange, John Smith hadn't struck her as being the lavish type....

Miss Millie rambled on. "I don't think he has any children. At least, he hasn't brought any to see the house. Course, it's not in any condition to be showing off."

"Yet, sister. Yet. He's already spoken to Natty Burke and Amos Philbrick." Plumber and electrician, respectively. "I think he's starting at the bottom and doing it soup to nuts."

Pepper didn't have the heart to inform her that he was starting at the top, and it wasn't necessary. The point was the same.

"He's going to need plenty of fixin's to get that place in shape," Miss Millie scoffed. "Tom Fletcher was letting it go even before he moved out." She shook her head in a sparse gesture of disdain. "Waste of good land, that's what it is. A waste."

"But there's someone on it now, Millie. He's going to fix it up to look like it did when Tom's Rebecca, rest her soul, was alive." Miss Sylvie sat back in her chair with a pensive smile. "Do you remember that, sister? It was such a stately house."

Stopping her crochet hook for a moment, Miss Millie, too, sat back. "Oh, yes. That it was. Course the trees weren't so tall then and you could see the house from down the road. It was a credit to this town, the Fletcher place in its day...."

Handing the Thompsons their mail, Pepper left them to their nostalgia and proceeded along her route. Again, neither Shaw was home, but she rarely saw them except on Saturdays. Mrs. Biddle, on the other hand, was home and ready to talk.

"And what do you think of our new neighbor?" she asked as she took her mail from Pepper.

"Nice guy."

"Mmmm." Mrs. Biddle studied her for a moment. "How old are you, dear?"

"Twenty-seven."

"Twenty-seven and dreaming of having a husband." Pepper was about to contradict her when she went on. "You'd make a wonderful mother. I've seen you with little Chrissie." Mrs. Biddle smiled. "Isn't she an angel?"

Pepper's lips twitched at the corners. "I can't argue with you there." Lest she argue with Mrs. Biddle on that other score, Pepper conscientiously departed. Yes, there was part of her that wanted a child, wanted one badly. She'd held Chrissie, had felt the little arms curve around her neck, the warm body curl into her, the butter-soft cheek brush her own. Children had so much to give and they gave it wholeheartedly. If she ever had a child, she'd never betray that trust.

But then, she would never have a child, because she didn't have it in her to make love with a man. She couldn't indulge in that kind of commitment. Commitments were made to be broken. Love didn't last. And she couldn't bear to be hurt again.

John Smith was on his roof. As she caught sight of him, Pepper's bitter thoughts vanished. He looked very much the same as he had the day before, all sweaty and bronzed. She wondered how long he'd been working, wondered whether he was an early riser, too.

"Morning!" she called out, her stride steady. She wanted to call him John, but wasn't sure if she should. Yet "Mr. Smith" seemed far too formal for the man, and he wasn't that much older than she was to warrant the formality as was the case with, say, Mrs. Burns and Mrs. Biddle. Old Sam was something else; no one called him anything *but* Old Sam, unless in an epithet behind his back.

"Hi, Pepper!" Setting down his hammer, John came down from the roof. Pepper made no attempt to stop him as she'd done the day before; she sensed she'd be wasting her breath.

As soon as his foot hit the ground, he reached for a towel he'd slung over the porch railing and mopped his face, then his chest. Pepper followed the action, noting that his chest hair gleamed against his tan.

"Doesn't it hurt your, uh, your feet . . . working barefoot up there?"

Draping the towel around his neck, he shook his head. His cheeks were smooth; he'd obviously shaved that morning. She wondered if he usually did it at night when he cleaned up from work, as many manual laborers did, and further wondered why he'd switched his schedule from yesterday. But then, she cautioned, who was she to question? Didn't she usually bathe at night?

"It's easier, actually," he answered, and it took Pepper a minute to recall her original query. "The traction's better because I can feel exactly where I am. And I like the freedom. Fresh air. It's warm enough without wearing heavy work boots. Speaking of which—" He ducked around the porch and turned back with two cans of soda, which he'd drawn from the cooler. Popping the tab on one, he handed it to Pepper before she could refuse.

"Thank you," she said, her smile soft. She tried to forget the sliver of white briefs she'd seen above his cutoffs when he'd reached for the soda, but the image remained, doing weird things to her insides. Tipping the can, she took a drink, then watched as he opened the second can and quenched his own thirst. His neck was firm, strong without being thick. His Adam's apple bobbed gently as the cool liquid slid past.

"Hope Sprite's okay," he said, lowering the can and sinking onto a step. Legs extended, he lolled back, bolstering himself on his elbows. When he gestured toward the step in quiet invitation, Pepper accepted. She slid down at right angles to him, resting her back against a rickety banister that creaked under her slight weight. Her legs were tired, she told herself. She deserved a break.

"Anything's fine…as long as it's not Dr. Pepper." She gave a lopsided grin. "People love it. 'A Dr. Pepper for Pepper.' Let me tell you, it gets pretty tiring, especially since I hate the cherry taste."

John wasn't thinking of cherries. He was trying to place the light scent she brought with her. It was definitely floral, not fruity, and was just sweet enough for temptation. He cleared his throat. "I'll have to remember that." He took another drink. "Is Pepper a nickname or the real thing?"

"The real thing, I'm afraid."

"Why afraid? It's a super name."

"It's a flaky name." She shrugged. "I suppose it's better than Sunshine or . . . or Chastity. I'll never understand why some parents give their children such bizarre names. It's not as though the parent is the one who's stuck with the name for life."

"Pepper's not bizarre. Or flaky. It's . . . individual. Your parents must be spirited people."

She thought about that for a minute, then offered a quiet, "I suppose . . . when I was born," before putting her head back and taking another drink.

"Do they live around here?"

"Here? Oh, no." Then she qualified her denial. "Actually, I was born in Maine, but we moved away when I was little more than a toddler. I grew up in New Jersey."

John nodded. "Fine place," he said in such a tone that she sensed she didn't have to add a thing. "Are they still there?"

"Who?"

"Your parents."

"No. My mother's dead, and my father is—" this time it was a single shoulder that shrugged "—somewhere."

Noting the shrug and the accompanying chill in her voice, John filed them for later consideration. There was more immediate information he wanted. "Then you live alone?"

She held her voice steady. "Yes. Well, only in a way. I rent an apartment from a couple on the other side of town. They converted their old garage into a studio. It's perfect for someone like me."

"Small and fit for one?" he prodded as subtly as he could.

"Yes."

"But the couple lives in their house nearby."

"Uh-huh. Twenty-eight feet away, to be exact."

"That's good."

"Why good?"

"Someone your age shouldn't be alone."

Her laugh held more than its share of bitterness. "I've been alone for as long as I can remember."

Filing the bitterness, he concentrated on her age. He'd half hoped she'd pick up on that part of his comment and indignantly insist she was old enough for anything. Evidently he'd been *too* subtle.

"That long?"

"That long."

"How old are you, Pepper?"

He was the second person to ask her age that morning. She didn't mind the question. She knew she looked younger than her years and had nothing to hide. "Twenty-seven."

John tried to curb his surprise, then relief. "That's old," he managed, as though it were a rueful admission.

"How old are you?"

"Thirty-eight."

"Now that's old," she teased, eyes twinkling in a way that made John feel half his years, at best. She rested her head against the banister post and studied him through half-slitted eyes. "So, what's an old man like you doing in a place like this. Early retirement?"

John chuckled. She decided she liked the sound. It was not so deep as to be ominous, not so tight as to be studied. Just very natural, very comfortable—the kind of sound that warmed the soul.

"Not quite. I've taken a job up here."

Her teasing mood persisted. She felt decidedly light-headed and might have wondered if he'd put something in her drink had she not heard the snap of the tab herself. "Renovating houses?"

His lips turned down in that smile she found so unique. "Heading the guidance department at the high school."

"Guidance." Pepper sat forward and eyed him askance. "You're pulling my leg."

Reaching out, he did just that in a short little tug that brought her right foot inches closer. "Only now that you mention it." He left his hand around her ankle. It was slender, warm through the fabric of the dark gray knee socks that were part of her uniform. "I am, truly, a guidance counselor."

"Interesting," she managed, but her mind was on the fingers that held her ankle in a light clasp. His touch seemed as natural as everything else about him, devoid of either possessiveness or suggestion. She attributed the tingling of her skin to the warmth of the day and forced some Sprite down her throat. By the time she'd lowered the can, she felt more balanced. "Have you been doing it long?"

"Counseling? Since I graduated."

"You must love kids. Where were you working before?"

"In the city."

She should have guessed. Postmarks spoke volumes. "New York."

"Uh-huh."

"With the lavender lady."

John tempered his amusement, though his gray eyes danced. "She lives there, but, no, I didn't work with her."

Did you live with her? Pepper wanted to ask but couldn't. Instead, she gave a single nod. He knew what she was getting at; she could see it in his eyes. And she didn't want to sound overly curious. Not that she was, she told herself. What he did with his love life was his business.

"So," she began with a deep breath, "you've got the summer off to whip the old homestead into shape."

"Yup." Lifting his hand from her ankle, he grabbed the railing and hauled himself to his feet. "Have you ever seen the inside?"

"No."

"Come on. I'll give you a tour."

Pepper stood, but not to join him. "I really can't," she said quickly. "I'm supposed to be on the job. Lord only knows what they'd say if they knew I'd been drinking." She held up the can of Sprite, then took a final swallow.

"Me thinks they'd say you were a perfect rural carrier making a newcomer feel right at home."

His gaze held hers. It wasn't leering, as had been the looks of so many of her customers at the pub in Atlanta, or suggestive, as had been the expressions of far too many of the men whose cars she'd pumped gas into at the Texaco station in Philadelphia. Rather it was warm and sincere and exquisitely gentle.

Tearing her eyes from his with great effort, she looked down at the empty can of Sprite, then held it out to him. "Thank you," she said, encompassing both the drink and his kindness in her words. "It's been a nice break."

John took the can, then glanced down at her feet. "What do *they* say about those?"

She followed his gaze. "My Adidas? Oh, well, there was really no problem. Things are very casual up here. We drive our own cars. Even uniforms are optional. I chose to wear one because it's . . . fun. When it came to shoes, though, I assured the postmaster that I'd be that much more fleet footed in sneakers." She laughed and started to back away, determined to quit while she was ahead. "Of course, fleet footed is one thing. Sitting for half an hour on someone's front step is another. Oops." She stopped. "Damn. You're not good for my work at all." For the second day in a row she'd forgotten to give him his mail.

John Smith didn't look at all disturbed. "That's okay. You can carry it with you awhile, then come back for another drink later."

She handed him the mail. "And have every one of the neighbors snickering? They see everything, y'know."

John didn't care. "How about lunch? You can give me some tips on Naples's hot spots."

But Pepper was on her way again. "Hot spots? In Naples? If it's hot spots you're looking for, you've got the wrong place, bud."

He didn't want hot spots any more than Pepper did. He'd had his fill of them in New York and had come to Maine in search of peace. What he wanted was a peaceful hour or two with Pepper MacNeil.

"I could meet you somewhere . . ." he called to his rapidly receding mailperson.

She simply shook her head, held up a hand to wave without turning, then disappeared.

John might have been more discouraged had he been back in New York. There life was fast, time at a premium. Here, though, things moved slower. A leisurely enjoyment of small pleasures seemed to be the rule, if the people he'd met were representative.

Pepper was one of them, although by choice rather than birth. She was calm and easygoing. Oh, yes, he sensed a deep emotion beneath her surface. But he'd get at that slowly, savoring every brief foray. Hadn't she shared a cold drink with him today, while yesterday she'd refused?

He looked down at the empty can she'd handed him, then on impulse raised it to his lips and tipped his head back. One drop, then a second slid into his mouth. He let them linger there, feeling a kind of intimacy with the woman whose lips had touched the same spot on the can.

Someday, perhaps, he'd share a glass of wine with Pepper, then kiss the mellow moisture from her lips. Someday, perhaps, he'd touch her as he ached to do, bury his face between her breasts, breathe deeply of that light, sweet scent that even now lingered to tease him. Someday, perhaps. . . .

THAT EVENING Pepper dragged Pam Hoffman to the French film showing at an artsy theater several towns away. Though Pam complained about the subtitles, Pepper was in her glory. She was fluent in French. The film exhilarated her.

Two years older than Pepper, Pam was the local librarian, a divorcée who'd grown up in nearby Denmark, spent her college years and those of her marriage in Boston, and who had returned to Maine when her marriage had broken up. She and Pepper had met at the library shortly after Pepper arrived in Naples. They'd been good friends ever since.

Over hamburgers after the movie, they talked, sharing stories about locals whom they'd both encountered. Pepper was slightly taken aback when Pam mentioned John Smith.

"Then the other afternoon this magnificent thing walked in. I'm telling you, Pep, I've never seen anything like him. He was wearing a blue shirt and white slacks, almost preppy looking—" she struggled for the right words "—but very. . . with it. You know what I mean?"

"I know," Pepper answered with such certainty that her friend grew alert.

"You've seen him?" She stretched a hand up. "Real tall, sandyish hair, nice tan, super eyes—"

"And a smile that does its own thing? I've seen him. He lives on Casey Lane, which happens to be the only part of my route that I walk."

"Oh, Pep, are you lucky. You get to see him every day."

"He's just another postal patron," Pepper replied a little too blandly. "What was he doing in the library?"

"The usual." Her friend grinned. "Taking out books."

"On...?"

"Carpentry. Home improvements. Funny, he didn't look like the typical laborer."

You've never seen him bare chested. "He isn't. He bought the old Fletcher place and is doing it over. Come fall he'll be head of guidance at the high school."

A bulb lit in Pam's mind. "John Smith. No wonder the name I typed on his card looked familiar." She laughed. "I mean, that name *has* to look familiar. But now that you mention it, I do remember reading about his appointment in the paper." She tried to recall what she'd read. "He's from...New York?"

"Yup. One of *them*." She growled the last with such feeling that Pam was instantly on her case.

"Uh-oh. Your bias is showing. City boys aren't that bad."

"I'm amazed you're so forgiving."

"Hey, Joel was a nice enough guy. It was his mother who doomed our marriage. She wouldn't let go. But that's not to say *all* city boys have the same problem. Is he married?"

"Who?"

Pam shot a glance heavenward. "John Smith."

"No. But he's got a sweetheart who sends love letters drowned in lavender."

"Pepper! Be kind!" Pam lowered her voice. "Anyway, how do you know they're love letters? I mean, I know you guys read postcards, but . . . more than that?"

Pepper scowled. "No, Pamela. We do not steam letters open and read them on the sly. But, hell, this one reeked so, and the script was almost as flowery. Red ink, no less."

"I do believe you're jealous."

"Jealous? Me? Don't be absurd!"

Pam sat back, grinning smugly. "It's not absurd. He's a fine looking man. Just about the right age. And available."

"He may be, but I'm not."

"Is that why the two of us are sitting here . . . because we're so deluged with male companions that we seek solace in each other?"

"Tell you what, Pam. *You* can have him."

"Without a fight? That's no fun."

"The fun starts when he begins to analyze you."

"Analyze! He's a guidance counselor, not a psychiatrist."

"Same difference. They're both into reading minds, searching souls, digging up dirt that's irrelevant."

Pam was suddenly serious. "You sound defensive, Pep. Have you got all that much to hide?"

Pepper kept her tone even. "Of course not. It's just that I'm happy here. I like Naples. I like my job. The 'why' of it all isn't important."

Pam studied her friend. She knew the bare bones of Pepper's background and had often asked herself those very "whys." "Isn't there one part of you, even a tiny part, that would rather be teaching French at the high school? It's what you're trained for."

"I like the freedom I've got."

"What you're saying," Pam offered gently, "is that you don't want a job that'll tie you down for any longer than you want to stay in one place. If you decided to leave Naples, you could resign your job tomorrow and be on your way."

"I wouldn't do that. As I said, I like it here."

"Today. Maybe tomorrow. But next week? Next month?"

Pepper grinned. "And miss your making a play for John Smith? No way."

Sensing that her friend had just closed the door on one particular discussion, Pam accepted defeat with a smile and deftly changed the subject.

Pepper, on the other hand, thought long and hard that night on the probability of Pamela's making a play. True, Pam was divorced, as, according to Miss Sylvie's Ed Walsh, was John Smith. In that, they had something in common. But Pam wasn't right for John. Pepper knew it. For one thing, she was too short; she'd get a stiff neck looking up at him. For another, she was too fair; she'd burn to a crisp sitting on the front steps for even *half* a soda. For another, and another... Pepper found a million reasons why it was a bad match.

When she finally fell asleep, it was with the absurd conviction that she'd settled a troublesome matter.

JOHN WASN'T ON THE ROOF when Pepper walked up his drive on Wednesday morning. She could understand why; the sky was overcast, the slate-hued clouds threatening. Indeed, she'd driven her route more quickly than usual in hopes of beating the rain.

A single drop hit her head. She glanced up and quickened her pace, taking the steps at a trot. When she reached the front door, though, she stopped. And looked.

No mailbox. No slot in the door. She looked back over her shoulder, wondering if she'd missed a rural box he might have set at the end of the drive, but all she saw for the effort were several more large raindrops.

A doorbell? There was none. Her lips thinned in dismay. Raising her hand to knock, she paused. She didn't want to do this. It would have been so much easier to simply leave the mail and run. But leave it...where? On the front mat? No front mat. On a chair by the door? No chair. On the splintered wood that comprised the floor of the porch? If indeed it started to pour, the rotted overhang would do nothing to shield his mail from a soaking.

With a deep breath, she lowered her knuckles to the door. Once. Twice. Then she waited. When there was no response, she rapped again, louder this time and with mild irritation. If he expected to get mail, she reasoned, he should have an appropriate receptacle for it. She'd tell him that. *If* he was home.

She wasn't sure whether she was hoping for that or not when the sound of footsteps from within made the issue moot. She scratched the back of her left knee with her right sneaker. Her heart beat faster. A quick glance to the side told her the rain was truly beginning. She'd hand him his mail, turn, and make a run for the car. Real fast. No chitchat.

The door opened and she looked up to find John wearing that devastating smile of his. He was also wearing a T-shirt and jeans. Neither was baggy or dirty. He looked good. Too good. She was grateful for the screen door that separated them.

"Hi, Pepper. I'm sorry if I kept you waiting. I'll have to install a doorbell one of these days, I barely heard your knock."

"What you could install is a mailbox. Then I wouldn't have to bother you."

"You're annoyed."

"I'm practical. It'd really be much simpler, y'know. A little brass slot in the door...or a nice box mounted right here...."

"You are annoyed. I'm slowing you down." He'd been determined to watch her, but she was earlier than she'd been on the two previous days. "You're hurrying to beat the rain."

She cast a rueful glance behind. "There's no way I can, it seems. It was bound to come sooner or later." Lifting his mail from the top of her pile, she held it out, moving to the side to allow for the screen door opening.

John took not only his mail but her hand. Before she knew it, she was inside his house. "I've really got to run—"

"You're early. And it's coming down pretty hard now."

She could hear heavy spatters on the roof, the ground. Or was that her pulse throbbing through her veins? She wasn't sure. Nor did she have time to decide. Tossing his own mail on a low table just inside the door, he followed it with the rest of her load and took her hand again.

"Come. I'll show you the house."

She was about to argue when she reminded herself that rudeness simply wouldn't do. He was, after all, just another postal patron. It was his tax money that paid her rent.

She followed him—without choice, since he held her hand firmly in his—through the large front hall and off to a mammoth room on the left.

"The living room," he announced, giving Pepper time to assimilate the oversized windows, the marble fireplace. "It needs as much work as the rest of the place. I mean—" he gestured with his free hand "—the wallpaper's falling off and the floor's pretty battered. The windows are filthy and the molding's chipped. I have managed to clean the mantel."

"I can see!" she exclaimed, awed by the room even though she was aware of its disrepair. "The marble is magnificent."

John grinned, relieved at her enthusiasm. "It was one of the things I first noticed in the house. The guy who built this place—"

"Fletcher?"

"No, I think it was a man named Prince who came before him. He must have had a vision of what he wanted. Each room has something special. In here it's the marble." Tugging her along, he recrossed the hall to the dining room. "In here, it's the chair rail. Isn't that craftsmanship amazing?" Before Pepper could agree, she was being led into a smaller room off the dining room. "The butler's pantry. Can you believe a double sink in here *and* in the kitchen?" He tossed his head toward the room just beyond.

Charmed by his eagerness, Pepper teased, "Are you in the market for a butler?"

"Would I want a butler? Me?" His chiding laugh was ample answer. "Come look at the kitchen." He pulled her through. "It's got to be completely redone, but look at the size of it!"

"It is in proportion to the rest of the place," she offered, tongue in cheek.

"I'm going to tear out that wall and put windows in. That way I'll catch the morning sun."

"You are a morning person."

Acknowledging her statement without comment, he pointed toward a door. "There's another storage area, then the back door, and beyond that a mud room, then the door to the garage. Come."

They passed through a small corridor back to the front hall. A right turn brought them down another corridor to a more intimate, paneled den.

"This is unbelievable," Pepper exclaimed, leaving John's side to finger the fine wood that covered three walls and formed floor-to-ceiling bookshelves on the fourth. "Ah, books." Indeed, open cartons lay to the side, some empty, some only half so. "So you *did* bring something with you. I was wondering if you had any furniture." She sought John's gaze, finding it warm, happy.

"What I've got is in storage. Most of it, that is. Not that there's much, coming from a city apartment and all. I was hoping to buy stuff little by little."

Pepper nodded, wondering at the happiness she felt here. Moments before she'd been testy, annoyed that the man hadn't bothered with a mailbox. But his excitement was contagious. Her eyes made another circle of the room, pausing at a set of double doors. Approaching, she put her nose to the dusty glass.

"What's out here?"

"A porch."

She couldn't see much more than a metal framework. "Weird porch."

He laughed and joined her at the doors, gently pulling them open. "It needs new screens and an awning. I think I'll get to them next week. Look at the floor."

"What's under the rain?"

"Flagstone." He glanced up. "Come to think of it, maybe I ought to get the mop and start scrubbing while it's raining. Instant rinse water."

"Instant chill." She shivered, realizing she'd have to go out in that mess all too soon. "Maybe it'll let up," she murmured. "I really should get back to work."

"But you haven't seen the upstairs," John protested. When she looked up at him, he stared, then smiled. His voice was much softer when he spoke. "You've got dirt on your nose." He touched the spot, slid his finger over it.

Pepper held her breath, unable to believe that the tip of her nose was so sensitive. She wasn't aware that John had moved, yet suddenly he was closer. His warmth enveloped her. Even when he raised his hand from her face, she was held captive by an invisible bond. Then the hand returned, not to rub dirt from her nose, but to lightly caress her cheek. His fingers stole into her hair; his palm shaped her jaw.

She looked up to find his gaze on her lips. She bit the lower one. When, with an almost imperceptible movement he shook his head, she released it.

Then he lowered his head and she feared what was coming. She wanted to pull back, to turn, to escape. But her legs wouldn't work. It was as though the frenzied pump of blood through her veins robbed her of all other ability to move.

His lips grazed the tip of her nose, the fine line of her cheekbone. They felt cool against her warm skin, gently soothing. Pepper felt as though she was floating. Unknowingly, she closed her eyes to more fully appreciate the sensation. It was one she'd never known before, a kind of elevation. Oblivious to the danger of falling, she tipped her head to the firm texture of his mouth as it lightly kneaded the surface of her skin.

"You smell so good." His voice was a rough murmur, doing to her insides the same thing his touch had done. It was silky, yet sandy, stimulating her senses. "What is it?"

"Hmmm?"

"That scent."

"Jasmine," she whispered, opening her eyes. "It's my favorite. I bathe in it." She felt the tremor that passed through him, though she was oblivious to the image she'd painted in his mind.

"Oh, God," he breathed unsteadily, then he slowly straightened, closed his own eyes and let his head fall back.

When his hands dropped, her head lolled for an instant before snapping erect. She took a step back. "I've got to get back to work."

"I know," he groaned.

Turning, she fled through the den, along the short corridor and into the front hall. Where she found the presence of mind to retrieve her mail, she didn't know.

"Pepper...?"

John's voice neared. She reached for the doorknob.

"It's pouring."

"I'll make a run for it."

"You'll get soaked."

"I think . . . that might . . . be nice."

"Pepper!"

Tugging at the door, she was through it before he could grasp anything more than the screen that rebounded in her wake. Chin tucked to her chest, body huddled protectively over the mail, she sprinted forward.

"Pepper!"

"Have a good day," she called between breaths as she ran. She didn't stop until she reached the Carsons', and then it was only for the instant it took to leave their mail. The other houses on the return side of Casey Lane met a similar fate. By the time she found refuge inside her Rabbit, she was thoroughly soaked and breathless. The knowledge that she'd worked off a bizarre tension was small solace for the hollowness that lingered in the pit of her stomach.

Taking her frustration out on her car, she angrily turned the key in the ignition, flipped on the windshield wipers, then, jerking the steering wheel all the way around, made a sharp U-turn and stepped on the gas.

JOHN WAITED all Thursday morning for Pepper to show up. The sun was bright; he was finishing up the roof. It was hard for him to work, looking over his shoulder every few minutes.

Ten o'clock came and went, then eleven. He wondered if he'd scared her off. Hell, he hadn't even kissed her. Not that he hadn't wanted to. Not that he hadn't come very close. But he'd controlled himself; he hadn't wanted to come on too fast. Pepper MacNeil was different from the women he'd known. If she said she was twenty-seven, he believed her. Yet there was something . . . unspoiled about her.

By noon he was hammering shingles with a vengeance. She had probably gotten a late start from the post office. Perhaps she had a particularly heavy load. What if she was sick, though? Or had had a mishap with her car?

He knew that he didn't have a right to worry, yet worry he did. She inspired that kind of thing, free spirit that she was. In the three short days he'd known of her existence, in the even briefer time he'd spent with her, Pepper had intrigued him. Even now he could smell her. . . .

Thinking she had come, he nearly lost his balance twisting around to look. But the empty drive below met his gaze. He'd only imagined her. Wielding his hammer with even greater fury, he wondered if jasmine was addictive. It had to be; he hadn't been as fixated on seeing a woman since he was thirteen and had a crush on his older sister's best friend. Then, he'd staked out the pathway leading home from school. He'd sat in a corner of the lunchroom, scanning the crowd. He'd monopolized the wing-backed chair in the living room from which he could see the two girls whenever they came and went.

Even with Marianne, things had been different. They'd met in college and had started dating. It was a comfortable thing to do, if lacking in starbursts and thunderbolts. When they graduated, marriage seemed the sensible choice. It took them six years to admit their mistake.

"Come on, Pepper. Show up!" he growled, securing the final shingle with a vicious thud. Then, tossing his hammer to the ground, he gathered up the extra shingles and climbed down the ladder.

The Sprite wasn't half as refreshing as it had been two days before. He downed half the can and was about to pour the rest in the bushes when a movement caught his eye. Looking up quickly, he saw the mailman approaching. The mail*man*. Will. The one who'd delivered his mail when he'd first arrived, while Pepper had been on vacation.

The older man nodded a crisp hello and held out several letters and a magazine, which John quickly took.

"Thanks. I haven't seen you in a couple of days."

"Nope. Just covering for Pepper again. She's off today."

"Is she sick?"

"Nope. It's her regular day off. She'll be working tomorrow and Saturday."

Taking a deep breath, John nodded. "Gotcha." Then, raising the letters to his head in salute, he turned and climbed the front steps. Only when he'd set the mail down inside the door and stood back, hands on hips, did he realize how relieved he felt. She wasn't sick. She wasn't hurt. And apparently he hadn't scared her off after all.

Saturday. Raising a finger to his upper lip, he brushed it back and forth. It'd be a risk. She could turn him down. But if he didn't let her . . . if he was just clever enough. . . .

Taking the winding stairs two at a time, he realized he felt better than he had all morning.

3

PEPPER'S DAY OFF was lovely. She drove into Portland to walk and shop. Though never a lavish spender, she splurged on a gauzy sundress whose pale mint-green hue captured her fancy. Knee length and strapless, it was held together by a broad connected sash that wound twice around her midriff and waist before knotting at the hip. The dress was cool, refreshing, summery. She couldn't resist it, or a new pair of strappy white sandals. Or a new release of Mahler's Ninth Symphony.

Propped in her love seat with both feet on the coffee table and a glass of fresh lemonade in her hand, she listened to the symphony when she got home, then again that evening.

She was full of enthusiasm when she returned to work the following morning. Mrs. Burns was at her front door, as pleasant as ever. Sally, trying to feed a squirming Chrissie, wanted a detailed description of her dress. Old Sam was in his backyard working in the vegetable garden, grumbling about the rabbit that had somehow managed to sneak under the chicken-wire fence. The sisters Thompson were in their rockers wondering if she'd heard that Sabrina Duncan had had her baby. Pepper hadn't. She was thrilled. Sabrina and her husband Don lived at the far end of town; she'd watched Sabrina through the entire pregnancy with open envy.

The Shaw house was quiet, as was, surprisingly, the Biddles'. Pepper guessed Mrs. Biddle had gone to visit her friend in Poland Springs, and she wasn't unhappy. She'd have that much more time to talk with John.

Tendrils of excitement curled in her tummy as she approached his drive. He was just another stop on her route, but he was a very, very pleasant one. He was easygoing, soft-spoken, intelligent and interesting. She couldn't even begrudge him his near kiss the other day; it flattered her that he found her attractive.

As for the danger, she'd thought that all out while she'd walked around Portland the day before. She was in control. She knew what she wanted and what she didn't want. John Smith was simply another man. There was no harm in her looking forward to seeing him in the course of her route. He made her day that much more delightful.

Turning onto his pebbled drive, she broke into a soft smile. He was on the ladder, high against the side of the house, scraping paint. His body was long, extended with his reach. She noted the brush of hair beneath his raised arm.

"Hey, you!" she called as she approached, not wanting to startle him into losing his balance.

He turned his head, then grasped the ladder and twisted around. "Hi!"

Pepper continued walking, reaching the base of the ladder just as he set his foot on the ground. She grinned.

"So you finally opted for sneakers." Without socks. His legs looked marvelous.

"Shingles are one thing, ladder rungs another." He reached for a towel and mopped his neck. "Have you even tried standing barefoot on a ladder? It's slow torture."

"I can imagine." She looked up. "You finished the roof. It looks good."

John didn't bother to look. He was happy enough with the view before him. "Thanks. I finished yesterday. Seeing as I slaved up there all morning just waiting for you to come. . . ."

There was enough of an accusatory drawl in his tone to make Pepper instantly contrite. "Oh, hey, I'm sorry. It was my day off. I should have mentioned it."

John gave her arm a quick sneeze. "No problem. I'm kind of slow on the uptake sometimes. I should have realized it when you didn't show at your usual time."

"Will sometimes takes a little longer, especially now. The population of the town nearly triples in summer. You did get your mail okay, didn't you?" she asked cautiously.

"Sure. There was nothing exciting in it, though. It smelled just like . . . mail." He winked.

Pepper swallowed. "So. You're getting ready to paint." The shutters had been removed and lay spread out on the lawn.

"I figure that's next. *If* I ever get the thing scraped down."

"You've got paint dust all over you." There were tiny chips in his hair, a fine sprinkling on his shoulders and arms. Without thinking, she reached out to brush some flecks from his chest, but she'd no sooner touched him than he caught her hand and pressed it to his hard flesh.

Their eyes locked for a moment of acute awareness. Then, as though burned, each pulled his hand away.

John cleared his throat. More than anything, he'd wanted to move her hand around on his chest. Her touch aroused him; he wanted more. But he'd caught that stunned look in her eye and hadn't dared push.

"What did you do yesterday?"

Pepper rubbed her right knee with her left sneaker. "I drove into Portland to shop. It was fun."

"All by yourself?"

"Sure. There's nothing worse than dragging someone with you from one place to the next. Inevitably the other person gets tired of watching you try things on and wants to be somewhere else."

"Did you buy anything?"

"A dress. And shoes. And a record."

"A record?"

"Mahler's Ninth."

His teeth were brilliant white when his lips turned down in a smile. "No kidding. You're into classical?" He would never have guessed it. Somehow he pictured her dancing to Hall and Oates or the Police. She was full of surprises.

"Uh-huh. I took a course in school and have been hooked ever since. That was what my vacation was all about. I went with a group on a two-week tour of the musical high spots of Europe."

He was impressed. "Was it your first time over?"

"Oh, no. I spent my junior year abroad. I try to get back every couple of years."

It wasn't exactly the image of her he'd had in his mind. He'd assumed she'd graduated from high school, but there was something about the way she said junior year abroad. . . .

"Where did you study?"

"The Sorbonne. I was a French major."

"French major." It occurred to him that she knew precisely what was going through his head and was enjoying herself. He cleared his throat again; it seemed to be becoming a habit when Pepper MacNeil was near. "*Where* were you a French major?"

"Vassar."

He nodded once. "Vassar." If that was supposed to explain everything, it didn't. "And you're working for the post office."

She grinned brightly. "Uh-huh. Of all the things I've tried, I like this best. You've got a great bunch of neighbors, do you know that?"

"I'm finding out," he murmured, more than a little perplexed. "How about you? You've probably met most of the townsfolk, what with your job and all."

"Mostly I deal with rural boxes. They don't have much to say. But it's a small town. And I'm the only regular carrier. I suppose I've seen most of the residents at one time or another."

"Have any friends?"

"Sure."

"Good friends?"

"A couple."

He gave himself a silent kick, which he would have directed at her had he had the guts. She was being purposely obtuse. "Any *male* friends?"

Pepper reached toward the mail on her arm, took John's and deposited it into his hand. "A few." She turned and started off, calling over her shoulder. "None that send lavender letters, though."

John watched her go, then shook his head and chuckled. He'd had plenty of experience with women, yet nothing had quite prepared him for Pepper. He wanted to think she was jealous of Monica, but he wasn't sure. There were times when she seemed flip, self-contained, unaffected; then others, such as when she'd touched him earlier and their eyes had met, when she seemed deeply touched.

Rapping the mail against his leg, he turned. Tomorrow was Saturday. If his plan worked, he just might find out where he stood.

JOHN WASN'T HOME. Pepper sensed it the instant she started up his drive on Saturday morning. She wasn't quite sure how she knew, she just did. Her spirits sank. She'd been looking forward to seeing him, particularly since tomorrow was Sunday and she obviously wouldn't see him then.

Her suspicions were confirmed when she climbed the steps to find that he'd installed a shiny new brass slot in the front door. Sticking out of the slot was a long gray envelope. Out-going mail. If he'd been home, he'd have given it to her in person.

With a sigh, she thumbed through her pile, exchanged the long gray envelope with his in-coming mail, then turned. She'd reached the bottom step before lifting the gray envelope.

No stamp. For that matter, no address. She came to a halt. On the front of the envelope, scrawled in a relaxed hand, was one word: Pepper.

Heart pounding, she tore at the flap and drew out a single matching gray sheet folded in thirds. She opened it.

I've gone to get paint. Wasn't sure if I'd be back in time to see you, much less get anything done by way of work. It'll be pretty lonesome here later. How about dinner tonight? Please check one.

Eyes wide, Pepper read the list of options:

You're a dirty old man. Get lost.
I have a headache.
I never eat.
I've already made plans.
Yes, I'd like that. I live at_____
and will be ready by _____.

Sinking down onto the step, Pepper set the letter on her knee. She shook her head in amazement. Oh, she'd had propositions before, but none like this! At the pub it had been a lecherous, "Hey, doll, how about you and me...?" and had usually been accompanied by a sweaty palm on her butt. At the gas station it took the slightly more subtle—though equally as unacceptable—form a smug smile and a "What's a beauty like you doing in a place like this? Why don't I take you away from it for a little while. How about tonight...?" At college there hadn't been all that many boys to worry about. When she'd done her housepainting stint, she'd simply been one of them. As for the toll booth, well, she'd been able to handle anything that had zipped through with ease. The old "My lover is a linebacker" worked every time.

She studied John's letter again. The man was adorable, he really was. Dirty old man? No way. She couldn't check that one. And she didn't have a headache. Did she never eat? He should only see her pig her way through a thick-crust pizza with the works.

Other plans? No, she had no other plans. True, she did have friends. There was Pam...and Jenna, an artist whose home-gallery was down the street from Pepper's apartment. There was Stan, who ran a printing company in town and had asked her out on more than one occasion. But Stan was...blah. And Rick, who owned the bookstore in nearby Bridgton, wasn't much better. Not that she was sorry. She wasn't looking for dates. She didn't need them. Never had. And no, she didn't have plans for tonight other than to spend a quiet evening at home listening to music.

She paused...and thought. He was so very nice. And interesting. And good-looking.... Why not!

Feeling lighthearted and strangely adventurous, she tugged a small pen from her breast pocket and, using the rest of the mail as a desk pad, printed her address on the first line, seven o'clock on the second. Her pen hovered over the letters, then lowered to jot a P.S.

"If you overfeed me, I may never eat again. If you ply me with too much wine, I'll get a whopper of a headache. And if you turn out to be a dirty old man, I'll make sure I've got plans for here on in. P.P.S. I'll be wearing my new sundress. No McDonald's, please."

Neatly refolding the letter, she put it back in its envelope, crossing out "Pepper" to make way for her carefully printed "John." Pocketing the pen with a flourish, she trotted up the steps and dropped the envelope through the brass slot, then, fleet footed indeed, loped forward to resume her route.

HIS KNOCK CAME AT SEVEN on the dot. Pepper gave a final look in the mirror, then turned and ran down the stairs from the loft to answer the door.

He wore a pair of loafers, tan slacks, which did justice to his lean hips, and a dark brown shirt whose short sleeves and white collar made her want to rave about his tan.

"Hi!" She smiled, mildly breathless.

For a minute John said nothing. He wasn't quite sure what he'd expected, certainly not this soft pastel vision. "You look . . . great!" he managed when finally he found his tongue. "I've never seen you in anything but your uniform."

"Stunning, isn't it?" she said dryly, referring to the uniform.

John nodded wholeheartedly, looking her up and down again. "I'll say."

Pepper blushed. "I wasn't talking about the dress."

He wasn't either...entirely. It was the body that filled the dress that made it so perfect. But that was the dirty old man in him speaking. It was the mild-mannered counselor who actually verbalized his thoughts. "You should have been. It's fantastic. So this was the purchase in Portland?"

"Uh-huh."

"Then the day was worth it—my not seeing you, I mean." With reluctance he forced himself to look beyond her. "Hey, this is nice."

Stepping back, she belatedly gestured him inside. "It's small, but I like it."

John had never seen anything as simple and sweet in his life. There was little furniture; a love seat, two hassocks and a small coffee table seemed to do it. Against the walls were planks of wood alternated with cinder blocks to form bookshelves. At the far end of the room was a stand-up kitchen, directly above which was the loft. Anything paintable was either white or yellow. Anything that could be upholstered was in similar colors, but floral. The curtains, billowy and pulled back to admit the sun, matched the throw pillows, which matched the fabric stretched in a frame on the wall, which matched her bed.

Dragging his eyes back downstairs, he smiled. "It's bright and charming. Like you." He stuck his hands in his pockets for lack of something else to do with them. The sweet scent of jasmine floated in the air. It was making him high; he knew it.

Pepper tipped her head to the side. "Thank you, kind sir. I'll have you know that it's not just *anyone* I show my home to."

"Then I'm doubly honored."

"Doubly?"

"You agreed to have dinner with me. I wasn't sure you would."

"What? And miss a freebee? I think I spent my last dime on this dress. Rural carriers aren't exactly rolling in wealth." Particularly when they save every free penny for trips abroad.

He wanted to ask why she did it then, but realized he'd sound mercenary. In fact he was simply curious as to why a woman who'd majored in French at Vassar would be delivering mail. But the time wasn't right. He didn't want to risk offending her.

"Then you must be hungry." He took her elbow in as light a grasp as he could without revealing his own very different hunger. "Come on. We've got seven-thirty reservations. I thought I'd appeal to your obvious sentiments. Is French food okay?"

She ducked for the purse that lay on the shelf nearest the door. "You just hit the jackpot."

"And my prize?"

"My undivided attention for the evening."

He grinned. "I think I can handle that."

Pepper was sure he could, though it seemed that the reward was mutual. If ever she'd hoped for an attentive companion, John Smith was it. From the moment they stepped out into the early-evening sunshine, she was enthralled.

It began when she took a look at the vehicle he'd driven and burst into laughter. "I don't believe it!"

"What?"

"Miss Millie. She mentioned the shiny new thing you drove around in. The way she said it, I pictured some sporty little car, a Mazda or something. It's a Scout! I love it!" She ran a hand along the four-wheel-drive's sleek white flank.

John opened the door. "Sporty little things aren't terribly practical up here, I'm told. Not that I've had a taste of mud or snow yet, but this thing's been a godsend in hauling supplies back to the house." He helped Pepper in, saw the door firmly closed and ran around to the driver's side. He was reluctant to miss anything she had to say.

"You got your paint okay?" she asked as soon as he'd slid behind the wheel, then didn't bother to wait for an answer but eyed him in amusement. "It was very sly, that note you left. Are you always as creative?"

"Only when I spend hours on a ladder with nothing else to occupy my mind."

"What would you have done if I'd told you to get lost?"

He started the Scout and carefully left the drive. "I'd have been crushed. I'm not a dirty old man. Really I'm not."

She laughed. "I know."

And she did know. Furthermore, he continued to prove it to her through dinner. The restaurant was quaint, candlelit and atmospheric. The food was light and delicately seasoned. The service was leisurely and unobtrusive.

Over wine and a shared order of escargots, they discussed John's appointment.

"How did it come up?" Pepper asked. "Were you actively looking to leave the city?"

"Increasingly, over a period of several years."

"You weren't happy?"

He searched for the words to express what he'd felt. "It's tough being a counselor in New York. The kids are a world in and of themselves. I mean, to a certain extent it's that way everywhere, but somehow in the city it's that much harder. You start out thinking you can really make a dent, then realize that for every dent you work out, another pops up."

"You're not just talking poverty."

"Not by a long shot. We had our share of wealthy kids, and let me tell you, some of them were really screwed up."

"Drugs?"

"Among other things. There was no class distinction when it came to crises. Rich, poor, it was always something." His expression said what his words didn't. Pepper saw a sadness, a kind of defeat.

"And it got to you."

"Yup." There was finality in his voice.

"You're sorry."

"Yes, I am. As frustrating as things often seemed, I think I did some good. But I'm tired. Sixteen years was enough."

"Lake Region isn't free of crises," she cautioned.

"Believe me, I know that. And I wouldn't want it to be. If I had to sit in an office waiting for students to come calling, or wander the halls in search of troublemakers, or, God forbid, shuffle papers all day, I'd go out of my mind. But up here there doesn't seem to be—" he paused, searching again "—the intensity there was in New York. The same problems do exist, but on a different scale. And they're handled very differently. That's where the challenge comes in for me now. I guess I just need the change."

One corner of his lips quirked, turning up as much as was possible, given its natural inclination to go the other way. "Y'know, part of me really feels guilty about leaving New York."

"You're escaping while they can't?"

She understood; he felt warmed. "Uh-huh."

"And the other part?"

"The other part," he said, grinning, "couldn't be happier. I'd been aching to move to the country for years.

City living, even aside from the work, can do lousy things for your blood pressure. The constant rush gets to you. Up here, well, things are different."

She knew; oh, yes, she knew. "Why did you pick Naples?"

"I've often spent vacations in New England, so I had a rough idea where I wanted to settle. When the job offer came from Lake Region High it was too good to pass up. Finding the house was the clincher." He paused to carefully remove a snail from its shell. "You never told me what you thought."

"About?"

"The house. Do you like it?"

There was just enough unsureness in his voice to make her response all the more positive. "I love it!" she answered truthfully. "It's elegant."

Relieved, he smiled. "Not yet. It needs tons of work."

Pepper dismissed his statement with a quick shake of her head. "But everything's there. The groundwork and all. The original workmanship is magnificent, not to mention the design. The whole house is stately. I can't think of a better word."

"Thank you. I can accept that."

"Now you'll just have to worry about filling it. Won't a place like that be lonely...all by yourself?" The thought had occurred to her more than once; she recalled Mrs. Biddle's belief that the yard was made for children.

"It may be. But I couldn't resist buying the place. The price was right and . . ." He paused self-consciously.

"And what?" she urged softly.

"Well, I've always had a dream . . . of owning a house like that." His dreams went far beyond the owning, but he wouldn't tell her that just yet. "For the time being, I'm busy enough. When everything's done, if I'm lonely, I'll just have to think of doing something about it."

The lavender letter. Of course. She nodded, feeling a pang of something along the line of envy. Whoever filled that beautiful house with John Smith had it made for life!

"Will you . . . will you get everything done before school starts?"

He chuckled. "I sure hope so. I have a feeling I'll be pretty busy come fall. I'll be teaching several courses for the first time."

"Teaching? Really?"

"Uh-huh. The region wants to experiment with some courses on interpersonal relations. So many of the kids grow up here and then rush off to the city, to colleges or jobs, and they ought to be prepared for what they'll find. I'll also be teaching a course on problems—dealing with parents, understanding the pitfalls of experimenting with drugs and alcohol . . . and sex."

"Oh, heavens," Pepper mumbled. "Tell me you believe it's a sin to kiss before you can vote."

John's laugh was throaty. "Not quite. I think sex is great. And inevitable."

She held her breath, seeing something very warm in his eyes that had little to do with high-school students. But it passed, and he went on, "Unwanted pregnancies are something else. Lots of the kids here marry young. I'm not sure a seventeen- or eighteen-year-old can handle the responsibilities of marriage. Many of them have kids right off the bat, too. If they're already married, that's one thing. It's their choice; who am I to say they're wrong? But being forced into marriage because of a pregnancy—or worse, being forced to set aside other plans because a child is on the way—is unfortunate. I think kids have to be more aware of the consequences of their actions. Not that I can provide them with birth control. But I can make them aware that it exists, that they do have a choice. If they choose to abstain until they're ready to face the consequences, so much the better."

"Killjoy," she teased, thinking how much she enjoyed seeing a young couple kissing on a street corner in town. Kids were alive, spontaneous. Though she agreed with everything John had said, she kind of admired that carefree state.

"Is that to suggest," John began, his brows arched in amusement, "that you were a wild thing as a kid?"

"Wild thing? Me? Never." It was the truth. From the first, she'd known the consequences.

"I can't believe it. A woman as spirited as you?"

"Oh, I'm not all that spirited. Well, not when it comes to certain things."

"Like?"

Love. And sex. But she didn't want to say that. Instead she sidestepped his question. "I guess I am spirited when it comes to work."

Gracious, if alert, John allowed her the sidestep. "You've been here for ten months. Where were you before?"

"In Boston."

"Carrying mail?"

"Oh, no. I was a toll collector on the turnpike."

"A toll collector!"

"Sure, and before that—" she raised her eyes to the ceiling as though trying to recall everything in order "—I pumped gas in Phillie, and before that, I was a cocktail waitress in Atlanta, and before that—or was it after—no before, I painted houses."

"Why didn't you tell me?" he asked, struggling to mask his puzzlement with humor. "I could have hired you to help me out."

"I'm already employed. Besides," she said, tossing her head in mock arrogance, "I've put those days behind me."

"Hmm, and what's ahead of you?"

"Excuse me?"

"I was just wondering where you go from here. That's quite an employment record."

"For a French major? I can see right through you, you know." But she wasn't offended. Not in the least. There was nothing remotely critical in his manner. "You're wondering what a nice girl with a degree from Vassar is doing carrying mail . . . or pumping gas, or collecting tolls, or waitressing."

"Now that you mention it . . ."

"I like doing different things."

"And moving from place to place."

"Right."

"You don't want to put down stakes? Settle somewhere?"

She shrugged. "I like it here. Who knows? Maybe I'll go no farther."

They both pondered that while the waiter brought their dinner. Pepper had ordered duckling, John medallions of veal. It wasn't until their wineglasses had been refilled and each had had a chance to sample the succulent offerings before them that John prodded.

"You do enjoy carrying mail."

"Uh-huh. It's rewarding in ways some people would never imagine. A mail carrier—particularly in a town such as this, which only has one regular carrier—is attuned to the pulse of the community. In some ways the carrier *is* the pulse, passing things on from one resident to another. The residents come to depend on you; they see your coming as a vital part of their day. Even when I'm only delivering to boxes, you'd be surprised at the number of people I see. And the post office itself, well, it's a social center in its way."

"Do you ever get . . . frustrated?"

"Frustrated?"

"Not using your French. If you majored in it, you must have planned to use it."

Pepper carefully cut a piece of duckling from the bone and ate it. "Mmmm. This is good. Want a taste?" When he didn't refuse, she cut another piece and fed it to him. "I do use it."

John had completely forgotten what he'd asked. Was he the only one aware of the intimacy of being fed by a beautiful woman? He remembered the Sprite can he'd lifted to his lips. Maybe he had a fetish he'd never before realized he had.

"Use . . . your French?" he finally managed.

"Sure. I 'special-order' books in French. I go to French films. And when I travel, of course . . . Good, isn't it?"

She was talking about the duckling, but he couldn't begin to make an assessment. He barely remembered swallowing it.

"Great."

"How's your veal?"

"Not bad. Here." Maybe, he mused, she'd be affected if he fed her. He cut a small piece, extended it, watched her mouth close on his fork then withdraw. Her lips were soft, moist. He shifted in his seat.

"Mmmm. Delicious. Looks like we both lucked out. Or maybe everything here is well prepared. Amazing, isn't it, how a small restaurant in an out-of-the-way place like this can be so authentic?"

"Amazing." He sensed she was babbling and hoped for the best. Then, lest he press his luck, he backtracked. "Tell me what it was like . . . collecting tolls."

"Busy. During the rush hour or on holiday weekends we'd handle as many as three hundred and fifty cars an hour. I was in a forty-cent booth, which meant that I had to line up as many sixty-cent change piles as possible before I started. Two quarters, two nickels. Dimes wouldn't do since most of the drivers needed the nickels for later tolls."

"It must have been a treat for them—seeing you in a booth."

She shrugged. "I think it was my interview that got me the job. They told me they were looking for someone who could handle money, who was patient and courteous. I'd been a waitress, where those qualities were necessities. And you can bet I was courteous as hell during that interview. Actually, I was lucky at the Turnpike Authority; I managed to avoid the graveyard shift. I heard horror stories about that shift—you know, guys who rode through the booth over and over again, then waited for you to get off work."

"Did you ever have any trouble?"

"With pests? Nah. Oh, there were times when I'd be propositioned. There were some lewd comments." Her eyes twinkled. "There was a guy who rode through wearing nothing but a huge Greek cross. And the occasional one who didn't bother to stop." She laughed. "There was this guy who did it more than once."

"Did what?" John asked in alarm.

"Drove through without slowing down. He was older. Kept forgetting to switch out of cruise control. Then again, there were people I'd see day after day who were really pleasant. Some would tell you about themselves . . . what kind of work they did, where they were headed. They were lonely, wanted someone to talk to. It was only a problem when drivers behind them began to honk."

"Hmmm. That would be a problem."

"But they were nice. Really they were."

"Then why did you leave?"

For the first time she faltered, her eyes growing clouded for just an instant. They cleared so quickly, though, that he wasn't sure if he'd imagined the pause. "It was time to move on," she explained softly. "Like you, I wanted something quieter." She lifted her wineglass and took a sip, then put the glass down. "After a while, transiency gets to you."

"Are you talking about yourself or the people who whizzed through the toll booth?"

"Both," she admitted quietly.

"How did you pick Naples?"

"Much like you did. It was pretty. And I found a nice place to stay."

"Before you had a job?"

"I could have done anything," she offered lightly. "I think I might have enjoyed selling cosmetics at the local drugstore. Anyway, when I got up here I found that the rural carrier was retiring. Will, the substitute, wasn't interested in working full-time, so I had a shot at it."

"I thought postal positions were civil service."

"They are. What's a little test?"

He chuckled, knowing she'd score well on any test she chose to take. "And you got the job."

"I got the job."

"Are you planning on staying?"

For a time, at least. She never planned too far in advance. "Looks that way."

"I'm glad."

She was, too. This dinner with John was symbolic of the warmth she'd found in Naples. Even their conversation over dessert, less personal and dealing mostly with local politics and personalities, was a joy. When they arrived back at Pepper's place, she invited him in without a second thought.

"That dinner deserves a cup of my super-duper coffee." She opened the door and led the way. "Why don't you look through my record collection. Find something you'd like to hear."

What John really wanted to hear was the soft, kitten-like purr Pepper might make when he took her in his arms. He was sure she was a passionate woman; high spirit just oozed from her. Hell, she was twenty-seven and had had any number of exciting experiences. He was sure they had included men, though she hadn't mentioned any. She was being diplomatic, he knew, not talking of other men when she was with him, and one part of him respected her for it. The other part was damned curious. True, she seemed footloose and fancy free. But surely over the years someone had tried to stake his claim. Surely some man must have foreseen the kind of bright-eyed joy she could add to his life?

Her record collection was large and impressive, as was the stereo set she'd carefully arranged on its own broad shelf, its speakers correctly placed in the room for maximum enjoyment. She must have splurged, he decided, then realized that though she didn't have a large number of belongings, those she had were all of fine quality.

He chose a Dvorak Violin Concerto that he'd heard performed by the New York Philharmonic the year before. When he tried to remember whom he'd taken to the concert, he drew a blank. Joan? Or . . . maybe Deirdre? The fact that he couldn't remember was a statement in itself. Somehow he doubted he'd ever forget anything he did with Pepper. She was so different. . . .

"Here we go. I hope you don't like cream. I've only got milk, and it's vile when you're used to the other."

He turned to see her lowering a small tray onto the coffee table. "Black is fine."

She straightened, beaming broadly. "Ahhh, a gentleman of my own persuasion."

"Quite," he said intentionally, though he sensed his double meaning went over her head. No, not over her head. That would imply she hadn't understood. Rather, it was as though she could pick and choose what she wanted to hear. Anything of a slightly suggestive nature seemed to bounce right off her. Well, almost anything. He remembered her enthrallment when he'd brushed his lips over her face that day in his house. He remembered when she'd touched his chest—was it only yesterday?— and had been as stunned as he.

Taking the coffee she offered, he settled onto one end of the love seat. It didn't surprise him in the least when, slipping her sandals off, she curled one leg beneath her and settled beside him. Her knee was mere inches from his thigh. Dammit, why wasn't *she* twitching?

"Pepper, why aren't you married?" he heard himself ask and would have been appalled had it not been for the good-humored expression she wore.

"What kind of question is that?"

"It's a reasonable one," he said more gently. "You're twenty-seven and beautiful. You're bright, talented—"

"You mean I deliver the mail with a certain . . . flair?"

"You're laughing at me, and I'm dead serious."

"It's just that when you're dead serious you get this little line right here between your eyes." She touched the spot for a fleeting instant. "It makes you look older."

"I am older. And I'm wondering why no man has snatched you up before."

She stretched, then reached down to scratch the back of her knee. "Maybe because I'm not snatchable."

It was a flippancy at its best. He didn't believe her for a minute. "And what's made you so unsnatchable? An unhappy love affair early on?" Subtlety had gotten him nowhere. He desperately wanted some answers.

"You might say that," she murmured, then took a sip of her coffee. Finding it too hot, she set it back on the tray to cool.

"What happened?" John asked very softly. He, too, set his coffee down, but only so that he could give her all his attention. Stretching one arm across the back of the love seat, he turned to face her more fully. When his knee brushed hers, he didn't move it. He thought he sensed a tiny quiver in her, but she stayed where she was.

"Oh," she said on a sigh, absently fingering the soft folds of her skirt, "it's really past history. Nothing that a million other people haven't experienced."

He waited. When she didn't speak, he coaxed her in the most gentle tone he could find. "I'm listening."

She gave him a thin laugh and looked up. Her eyes held something he'd never seen before. Hurt. Pain. He felt his insides tighten. When she finally spoke, there was a meekness in her voice. "You must be very good at your job. I can't remember the last time I've talked so much about myself in one night."

"You haven't said all that much really. What I'm asking you now—_that's_ what I really want to know."

"You're going to dissect my mind."

"I'm not going to dissect your mind."

"You will. It's your profession."

"I'm a counselor. I try to guide people in positive directions. If they have problems, I try to help them understand and cope. I'm not a psychiatrist. I wouldn't know the first thing about taking someone's mind apart and presuming to be able to put it back together. Besides, I'm not here tonight as a counselor. I'm here as a friend, for starters. Now, tell me about the disaster that turned you off marriage."

Pepper felt suddenly sheepish . . . and afraid. She'd never shared much of her past with anyone. But John was different. He wasn't just anyone. He was her friend. And she was making a big deal over nothing.

"Oh, my parents split when I was young. That's all."

"And it was ugly?"

"Not really. Just . . . painful."

He moved his hand, very, very gently slid his fingers beneath her hair and began a light caress of her neck. "How old were you?"

"Seven."

"And you were aware of what was happening between them?"

"Between them? Not terribly. But I was aware that the man I'd idolized—the man who used to tote me around on his shoulders and read me good-night stories—was gone, and that he'd taken my little brother with him."

"Brother. I didn't realize you had any siblings."

"I don't. Not for practical purposes, anyway. I haven't seen either of them since."

"Not once?" He couldn't believe it. There were all kinds of divorce settlements, most of which would certainly have included visitation rights.

"Not once," she stated baldly.

Had she not mentioned her brother, he might have been able to accept it, if reluctantly. "Didn't your mother want to see her son?"

"If she did, she never told me. Once they were gone, she never mentioned their names again. It was as though they'd never even existed."

"God, Pepper, I'm sorry. Had you been close to your brother, too?"

"I adored him," she stated. What little emotion her voice held was tightly reined. She might have been talking of the weather.

"And you hurt?"

"Yes."

"What about your mother?"

"My mother closed up and barely gave a thought to me, much less to them. I was thirteen when she died. I wish I could say that I missed her, but we were never close, not once the others left. I don't think we ever had a good talk. I don't remember her ever holding me."

"Who did take care of you?"

"I did."

"When your mother died."

"A cousin of my mother's. She was married but had no children. Out of choice, I think. She wouldn't have known what to do with a child. Fortunately, I was pretty self-sufficient. She gave me room and board. I didn't need anything else. The little money my mother left me went into the bank for clothes, then gave me a start toward college. I won a scholarship; otherwise I doubt I'd have been able to finish. I'd worked since I could remember, so I was even able to manage the year abroad." Her voice grew stronger; she'd come through the worst. "Then, when I graduated, I had the ticket I needed. A kind of security."

"But you didn't do anything with it."

"In terms of occupation, no. There were too many other, different things I wanted to do."

"But none that involved marriage. Or love."

"No."

"I'm sorry," he said with such gut-wrenching feeling that her eyes sought his and she smiled.

"No need. I'm all right. Really I am." Strangely, she felt more than all right; she felt closer to John than she'd felt to another human being since she could remember. He was a friend, a good friend. His face was near, features strong. The warmth of his body reached out to comfort, to soothe. When he raised his free hand and stroked her cheek with the backs of his fingers, she tilted her head into them.

"Love can be very beautiful," he murmured.

"So can life. Even without love," she answered as softly.

"But something's always missing."

"No. When one expects nothing, each small pleasure is that much more meaningful."

"But when you don't *know* what you're missing . . ." he began, then let his words trail off as he lowered his mouth to hers.

4

PEPPER COULDN'T RESIST this small pleasure. It was a perfect nightcap for the evening, a perfect way of pushing from mind all that John's questions had dredged up. She'd been kissed before, but never with such gentleness, such feeling. Even the feathery touch of his lips on her face that day in his house couldn't compare in tenderness with what he offered her now. Perhaps it had to do with their conversation, with the closeness their time together inspired. Perhaps it had to do with something else, something deeper. But she couldn't think, could only feel, and she wasn't about to question something that felt so fine.

His lips stroked hers, lightly, firmly. The hand that had caressed her cheek now joined its mate in holding her face up for his pleasure and hers. He took her lower lip in his mouth and sucked on it, then did the same to her upper lip. She was floating once again, but higher this time and with no desire to touch ground.

"God, you taste as good as you smell," he moaned, showing her just what he meant. His tongue circled her lips, sampled their soft inner lining, traced the even line of her teeth until, relaxing an innate guard, she opened to him. There was no part of her mouth that he didn't touch then. Finally the sheer need for a breath drew them apart.

Scooping an arm under her legs, John shifted them over his. "Should I stop?" he asked, abundantly aware of a growing tightness in his groin.

"Oh, no," she whispered. "That felt good."

"Put your arm around me," he commanded. When she had, he pulled her more fully into his embrace. One arm circled her back, offering her the support he'd denied her when he'd drawn her forward. The other held her chin, fingers spanning her jaw.

His mouth captured hers again, lips wide. It was an elusive capturing, but a capturing nonetheless for Pepper could do nothing but conform to his will and that of her own nascent sensuality. Their lips barely touched at times, simply whispered softly, openly, as though to catch the other's breath the instant it emerged.

She ran her fingers through the hair at his nape and found it thick and warm, as appealing to her senses as was his coffee-tinged taste. She slid her other arm around his shoulder and basked in his strength. Eyes closed, she glided through a world strangely peaceful yet at the same time exciting in the way of something new and decidedly exhilarating. She felt very much at home in his arms.

When he buried his face against her neck, she hugged him tighter. "Oh, John," she whispered, in awe at the pleasure he gave her.

"Say it again," he whispered back. "My name. You've never said it before."

"Haven't I? I'm sure I have . . . in my mind, at least."

"But to me. Say it."

"John," she whispered. "It's a strong name . . . John."

He kissed her again then, more forcefully. She couldn't mind, he decided, because she'd begun to run her hand over the muscles of his back. When her fingers traced his spine, he struggled for control. It was as if the downward gesture went far beyond her fingertips, coiling through his lower torso to settle between his legs.

Gently pressing her back to the cushions, he kissed her closed eyes, then the freckles on her nose and the smooth line of her cheekbone. He ran his hands up and down her arms, finding her skin soft and warm. Slipping an arm beneath her neck, he offered her more of his weight and was rewarded by the sweetest sigh he'd ever heard.

"I'm not hurting you, am I?" he whispered.

"No, no," she breathed. "Still feelin' good." In truth, her body had begun to arch toward his, suddenly needing greater pressure to ease the vague ache that gathered below.

"Mmmm." His lips caught hers, the kiss fueling his hunger. He wondered why he'd never felt this way with another woman and imagined it had something to do with Pepper's freshness. One part of him knew she couldn't be inexperienced, the other part felt she had to be experiencing things with him for the very first time. It was an exciting thought and it nearly drove him mad.

His lips slanted hotly over hers as he slid his hand down her neck. He traced the hollow of her throat with his forefinger, massaging it while his other fingers spread wide over her chest. The gauzy fabric of her dress tantalized his wrist, but he explored her bare shoulders, shaping them to his palm, before moving lower.

The sound of surprise became one of pleasure in her throat when he finally covered her breast. Quite help-less to protest, Pepper found herself swelling to his touch. Her breath came faster; she couldn't believe the pleasure she felt. It was so very new and different, the antithesis of the furtive maulings she'd endured on occasion in the past, moments before she'd pushed the offending hand away. But there was nothing offensive in John's hand and she had no desire to push it away. Rather she strained to-ward it, thriving on its insistent pressure, craving more.

His fingers moved steadily, circling the firm mound, moving slowly inward until they reached her nipple. She moaned into his mouth, then again when he began an agonizingly sweet tugging.

But it wasn't enough for him or for her. Freeing the arm that had been beneath her neck, John propped himself up in a half-seated position and, eyes holding hers hyp-notically, slipped his fingertips, just his fingertips, be-neath the gauze bodice. Lower and lower he moved them on her willing flesh, giving her ample time to demur. But her eyes were alight, her lips slightly parted in the faintest smile of fascination. Encouraged by her obvious plea-sure, he eased the gauze down to her waist, leaving her breasts naked and incredibly beautiful.

"Oh, Pepper," he whispered hoarsely. His eyes ca-ressed her curves, noting the responsive puckering of her nipples. He touched one and she caught her breath, stunned by the shocklet of energy that sizzled from that small touch point through the length of her body to the very tip of her toes. She felt alive in ways she'd never imagined, alive and glowing.

"You're magnificent," he rasped, putting his hands on her ribs and moving them slowly upward. He seemed to need to touch every inch of exposed flesh and he did so, skirting her breasts with all but his eyes until she felt a searing ache for him.

"Please, John," she whispered with the little breath that was left her, "touch me . . . touch me." Covering his hands with her own, she urged them to her breasts, releasing them only to cling to his wrists when he began a tantalizing exploration of her engorgement. She closed her eyes and let her head fall to the side, concentrating solely on the heady feeling of his work-hardened fingers on her softer flesh. When he took her nipples between his thumbs and forefingers and rolled them, she moaned softly.

"Does that—" he began, but she cut into his expression of concern.

"No! No, don't stop. . . ." She was dizzy with desire, thriving in the fire he stoked.

He took her hands then and, anchoring them by her shoulders, bent his head to her breast. His tongue darted toward the pebbled tip, grazing it again and again until it grew almost painfully hard. His breath was warm on her bare flesh, making her shiver. The moisture he left on her nipple made her burn. Unknowingly, she turned her hips in to him, arching, seeking. He lowered enough of his weight onto her to satisfy her need—and his—

against his tumescence. Then he opened his mouth and enveloped a rosy-brown areola, sucking in a way that made Pepper writhe all the more.

"I need you, sweetheart," he moaned. "I need you." The steady undulation of his hips elaborated; Pepper met his movements, guided by instinct and a driving need of her own.

When he lowered a hand to slide her skirt up, though, she finally managed to grasp what was about to happen. It wasn't that she didn't want it, though deep down she knew that such a step couldn't be taken lightly. Rather, it seemed critical that she exert control, for her own sake if not for John's.

"Wait . . . John," she gasped, stilling his hand with her own. "I think . . . I'm sorry . . . I can't . . . yet . . ."

John went very still, every muscle hard. "You can't?" His voice was deep, almost gruff. With slight force, he pushed his hand beneath hers to the juncture of her legs. She gasped when he touched her and blushed with the knowledge of the dampness he felt. "You can."

"I know . . . but I don't want . . . I'm afraid . . ." She was afraid of losing herself, of relinquishing that control she'd held for so long. Did he realize that? Could he understand . . . and accept it?

Slowly he removed his hand, collapsing over her, burying his face in the cushion above her shoulder. His entire body shuddered. His breath came in rough drags, quieting reluctantly. When he finally spoke, he'd regained a semblance of composure. "You've nothing to fear from me, sweetheart."

It was the second time he'd used the endearment. In the many times she'd heard it in her life, not once had it held the meaning it did now. Sweet heart. His voice gave it a special lilt, a soulful legitimacy.

She ran her fingers through his hair in comfort. "I know," she whispered. "It's me. I...lose myself when I'm with you. But I can't.... I don't want to rush into things."

He sat up then and gazed once more at her breasts. He touched them in a lingering way as though to memorize their lush curves before he reached to tug up her dress. The soft fabric, having folded over on itself, resisted him. He cleared his throat.

"I think you'll have to do this. I don't know how it works."

The dull red color that rose to his cheeks minimized her own embarrassment. Sitting up when he stood, she struggled with the fabric herself. When it proved to be as stubborn as her own hand, she went to its source, the knot at her hip.

John moved away to stand, hands on hips, with his back to her. She released the knot, which in turn loosened the entire top half of the dress. Drawing the gauze up to cover her breasts, she rewrapped the sash and knotted it. Then, standing up slowly, she raised her eyes.

"You can turn around now," she coached, lips toying with a smile.

"I'm not sure I should."

"Why not?"

"Because I'll keep seeing you barebreasted—"

"I'm all covered up."

"Not in my mind."

"Does that mean you'll never look at me when I come to deliver the mail?"

He shook his head, snorted, then slowly turned. "Of course not." Closing the distance between them with three easy strides, he put his hands on her shoulders in a gentle caress. His warmth reached out, restoring her balance.

"I can't tell if you're smiling or frowning," she teased. "No halfway measures, please."

"I'm not sure which one I want to do."

"You can smile."

"When you've turned me down?"

"Oh, John," she said softly. Her hands found their way to his chest and stroked his shirtfront in a gesture of affection that was more consoling than sexual. "It's not you I've turned down. It's me." She looked away, strangely shy. "Don't you think I enjoyed myself?"

"I thought so. That's just it. These are the eighties. If a man and a woman feel—"

"What happened to the guy who was talking earlier against free sex?"

"I was talking about high-school students. We're adults. And I wouldn't call what we were doing—or about to do—free sex by any means. There's nothing irresponsible in my feelings toward—"

She put her fingers against his lips, fearing what he might say. "Shhh. Please. I don't want to argue."

He took a deep breath and sighed, looping his arms around her waist. "Neither do I. It's been too pleasant an evening."

At mention of the evening, she cast a glance to the side. "You haven't had your coffee."

"I think I'd better not. It'll keep me up all night. At the rate I'm going it's gonna be a long night anyway."

"I'm sorry."

"Don't be. I'll respect you all the more in the morning. . . . That's what I'm supposed to say, isn't it?"

She grinned, dazzled by his upside-down smile. "Uh-huh."

"Then—" he set her back "—I'd better be going before my good intentions are tested." Mindful that the next day was Sunday, he was about to ask her if she had plans, then thought better of it. He needed a day to cool off. She'd given him much food for thought. "Take care, y'hear?"

She nodded, savored the brief touch of his lips to her brow, then watched him walk to the door and let himself out. The door closed quietly behind him. She listened, putting picture to sound as his car door opened, then shut. The Scout growled awake, hummed as it backed around, then purred to full life when, with the shift of gravel beneath its tires, it took off.

The night's silence had long since been restored when Pepper sank back onto the love seat. Reaching for her cool coffee, she was about to take a sip when, on impulse, she set the cup down again and reached for the one John had used. Raising it to her lips, she rubbed them against its edge, took a slow, satisfying taste, then replaced the cup on the tray. Standing, she crossed to the stereo, studied the album he had chosen, removed the record from within and put it on. Then, feeling strangely happy, she returned to the love seat, stretched out on it and closed her eyes, letting the peace of the music fill that tiny void John's departure had left.

But she wasn't thinking of the void. Rather, she was thinking of the pleasure she'd felt in John's company, in his arms. And she was thinking that it might not be so bad to follow the yellow brick road and see where it led. As long as she remained in control of her emotions, she was in no danger whatsoever.

JOHN SPENT the next two days scraping down the rest of the house, then began the slow task of applying fresh paint to all but the brick front. He had his work cut out for him.

Though he thought often of Pepper as he worked, he contented himself with awaiting his mail everyday. He sensed that she needed room, that to crowd her would only turn her off. Fortunately, his hot-water heater was in need of repair, so cool showers were as inevitable as they were necessary.

When she came on Monday, they shared a cold drink and talked of the pros and cons of his paving the drive. When she came on Tuesday, he offered her a Popsicle, then had one himself as they debated the relative merits of black or navy blue for the shutters. When she came on Wednesday, he dragged her out back, poured her an ice-filled cup of sun tea and sought her opinion of the awning swatches he'd selected for the porch.

When she came on Thursday, he was surprised. It was her day off. He'd fully reconciled himself to merely dreaming for the day. When her bright voice called up to him shortly after he'd climbed his ladder and begun to paint, he couldn't quite believe she was for real.

"Need some help?" She was wearing a pair of shorts, an oversized T-shirt with Make Mine Mozart printed on the front and sneakers. Her hair was gathered off her neck into a high ponytail. She shaded her eyes against the sun.

"Pepper." He set down his brush and stared. "I don't believe it."

"What's not to believe? It's my day off and I've got nothing to do. I have had some experience in this line of work, if you'll recall."

He climbed carefully down the ladder, half fearful he'd miss a rung for wanting to look elsewhere. When he reached the bottom, that was just what he did. A broad grin lit his face.

"You look about sixteen years old. Where'd you ever get the T-shirt?"

She laughed. "I wish I could say in Austria, but I don't think they'd so dishonor one of their national heroes. I bought this in Boston." She glanced down and pulled the soft fabric from her chest. "Like it?"

"Mmmm." He liked it better when it clung, though even then it was loose enough not to wreak much havoc with his libido. Her bare legs were another matter. They seemed to stretch forever, and she wasn't overly tall.

"Well . . . ?" she prodded.

"Nice."

"Not my legs," she scoffed, aware of his line of sight. "Are you going to let me help?"

"Help?" Raising his eyes, he cleared his throat. "Uh...help. Sure. You really want to...on your day off and all?"

"I wouldn't be here if I didn't."

"Then you've got yourself a job, my girl," he said, jauntily throwing an arm about her shoulders and propelling her several feet before stopping.

"Where are we going?"

"Nowhere." He'd just needed to touch her. She fit well in the crook of his shoulder. "I'm...thinking." He raised a finger to his upper lip and stroked it. "We'll need another ladder." He frowned. "How did you get here? I didn't hear a car."

"I rode my bike."

"Your bike?"

"Sure. It wasn't far, and it's a beautiful day. Besides, the Rabbit needed a rest, even if I didn't. You don't have a second ladder?"

"Not at the moment. How about the shutters—want to do those?"

"The shutters are a pain."

"I know," he stated with proper disdain. He hated the thought of doing them almost as much as he hated the thought of Pepper balanced precariously atop a ladder.

"But it takes real skill to do shutters. Someone with your expertise could do the bang-up job I couldn't."

Pepper's smile turned lopsided and she gazed into the handsome features above hers. "You are a bull slinger if I ever heard one. And I know what you're doing—appealing straight to my ego. All right, I'll do your shutters. Did you get the paint?"

"The paint. Oh, hell."

"You didn't. Then it's a choice between driving into town for paint or a second ladder."

"Paint."

"What color did you decide on?"

"Navy."

"Mmmm. Good choice." She stuck out her hand. "Give me your keys. I'll take the Scout and pick it up while you go on painting—"

"Are you kidding? And miss the chance to take you for a ride?" He wiped his hands on his cutoffs, then grabbed her hand and headed for the kitchen. He left her there only long enough to run upstairs for a shirt and his wallet. Then he led the way to the Scout and they were off.

They stopped for breakfast in the center of town. Though Pepper claimed she'd already eaten, she managed to down an omelet while John had pancakes and eggs.

"See?" she quipped, sitting back in the booth to relax over the last of her coffee. "If I hadn't come along you never would have eaten. Don't you like to cook?"

"Not if I can help it."

"How have you survived all these years?" she queried, only then recalling something—was it one of the Thompson sisters who'd said it—about his being divorced. "Oh. You did have someone for a while."

"News travels fast." He was neither surprised nor upset.

"In a town like this, you bet. You're divorced."

"Uh-huh." He took a deep, satisfied breath, patted his still-lean stomach and sat back. "Are you curious?"

"Sure. What happened?"

"It died a slow death."

"No drag-em-out fights?"

"Nope."

"No kids?"

"Nope."

"What was her name?"

"Marianne. We married right out of college and were divorced six years later. The decision was mutual and satisfactory. We both knew we'd made a mistake, and since there were no children involved...."

"Has she remarried?"

"Uh-huh. She had three kids at last count."

"Didn't you want kids?"

"Then, no. Now, yes."

She ignored the faint palpitation in her breast. There was still the matter of the lavender lady, yet she couldn't ask. She veered off on a tangent instead. "What about your family?"

"My parents live in Harrisburg. Dad's retired; he was an accountant."

"And your mother?"

"Was—is—a mother. And wife. Women's lib didn't quite make it to her."

"You're very lucky," Pepper offered with a sincerity that made John feel the slightest bit guilty. He had been lucky; he'd grown up in a house filled with love, while Pepper had been robbed of it at a frighteningly early age.

"Do you have any brothers or sisters?" she went on, indulging in her curiosity while the going was good.

"One sister." His eyes took on a special gleam. "She's two years older than I am."

"Is she married?"

"Uh-huh. With three kids. All boys. She sees herself as the queen bee. But then, Monica's always been a little dramatic."

"Where does she live?"

"New York." He waited, wondering if Pepper would make the connection, but she seemed to take this new bit of information with the same wide-eyed interest as she'd taken the rest.

"Are you close?"

"We always have been. I'm hoping they'll be up in August to see the house. The boys are at summer camps farther north, and Monica and Greg thought they'd pick them up this year themselves, rather than letting them go home on the bus. Naples is right on the way. There was even some talk about dragging my parents along, although how they'll manage the return trip with four adults, three boys, miscellaneous trunks, duffel bags and air spray enough to cover the smell of mildew is beyond me."

Pepper laughed in delight at the picture he painted. "Sounds like fun to me."

"Not when the kids start fighting, let me tell you. I've been along on outings like those and they're hair-raising." But the softness in his eyes belied the claim; he loved his nephews, however they behaved. He knew that Pepper could see that. He also knew that she was envi-ous; a certain sadness deep in her eyes told him so. "Hey," he said, sliding from the booth and reaching for her hand, "at the rate we're going we'll never get anything painted. I can't afford to fritter away the offer of an extra pair of hands."

They picked up the navy paint, then headed back to the house to work. Pepper remained on the ground where she diligently sanded, then applied paint to the shutters. She found she had the patience of a saint when it came to working along each narrow slat, and she assumed it had something to do with the peaceful setting in which she worked. John was up on his ladder, his bronzed body hers for admiring. If she worked more slowly than she ever had, she attributed it to the frequent breaks John seemed to want to take.

Friday found her back on her route. She talked with John for a few minutes while he worked, then moved on. Come Saturday, she was half hoping that she'd find an-other note for her in the brass slot; it had been charming to be asked out that way.

But John was painting still. And there was no note.

When Jenna called late that afternoon and suggested an early dinner in Bridgton, Pepper readily agreed. Her apartment seemed strangely quiet and she wasn't in the mood for music. Besides, she enjoyed Jenna; it had been a while since they'd had a chance to talk.

Over salads and quiche, they shared their news. Pepper told Jenna all about her trip, filling her in on details as she proudly displayed the snapshots she'd taken. Jenna spoke at length about a new piece she was working on, the first of a silk-screen trilogy that she hoped would sell to the small businesses and larger corporations that seemed to be snatching up her work as quickly as it left the studio.

"Things are going really well for you, Jenna. I'm glad."

"So am I," Jenna groaned good-naturedly. "After years of nearly starving, of selling one picture at a time, things are picking up. The art consultant I'm working with is terrific. He travels all over New England placing artwork. If it weren't for him, I'd probably still be relying on intermittent sales at the gallery."

"Do you miss painting? I mean, working with watercolors and oils as opposed to silk-screening?"

"Sometimes I do. So after I finish each print series, I get out the old palette. The variety is nice, actually. With my silk-screen prints selling so well, I'm that much more relaxed doing the other. But how about you, Pepper? How's everything going?"

"Great. I'm enjoying the route."

"Not getting bored?" Jenna was well aware of Pepper's educational background and was as puzzled as Pam that she didn't itch to do something more.

"Nope. There's always something happening. Frank Moltz is moving. Did you know that?"

"Moving? Thank God. He's a jerk."

"Come on. Once you get past the cowlick, he's a nice guy."

"He's a jerk."

"Is he still asking you out?" Pepper asked.

"Once a month, at least. You'd think he'd get the hint."

"He must have, if he didn't tell you his plans, though I think he only made the decision this week. I heard it from Judy Zarro who heard it from Frank's sister."

"Ahhh, the grapevine. Speaking of which...." Jenna cleared her throat.

"Yes...?"

"I understand you've been seeing someone."

Pepper's pulse jumped. "Someone?"

"Y'know, tall, tanned, sandy-haired...breakfast in town...."

"Mmmm. The grapevine."

"Well? Give."

Wearing a smug smile, Pepper turned the tables. "You give. What does the grapevine say?"

"That his name is John Smith—can't believe it—and he'll be at Lake Region High come fall."

"The grapevine's right on the button. He's a guidance counselor."

"Interesting. What about you?"

"What about me?"

Jenna rolled her eyes and mumbled under her breath, "It's like pulling teeth." Then she raised her voice and spoke each word with care. "Are you seeing him?"

"Sure. Every day. He's on my route."

"That's not what I mean, and you know it. Are you dating?"

Eyes wide, Pepper scanned the table. "Does it look like we are?"

Jenna shook her head. "You're too cool, Pepper MacNeil. Something's up. Did you or did you not have breakfast with the man two days ago?"

"The grapevine's precise, isn't it?"

"Pepper . . . ?"

Pepper frowned. "Yes, I did. But there's nothing going on. It was my day off and I'd offered to help him paint his shutters. He needed to buy paint, so we stopped for breakfast. He's a nice guy. That's all."

Jenna sat back, momentarily satisfied. "That's a start."

"It's the start of nothing. You know how I feel. I'm not looking for any kind of involvement."

"Sometimes you don't have to look to find it. Sometimes it falls right at your feet."

"But I don't want it, Jenna, therefore it won't happen."

"That's what they all say," Jenna quipped, but her smile faded at Pepper's look of consternation. "Why so vehement, Pep? Would it be so horrible to catch a guy like that?"

"I'm not looking to catch anyone. My life is just fine as it is. Besides, he's got a love in New York."

"Oh. So why's she in New York?"

"I suppose she's waiting till the house is fixed up." Funny, John had mentioned his sister's family coming up, perhaps even his parents, but he'd made no mention of the lavender lady. Then again, of course he wouldn't. Not while he was with her. He was too much of a gentleman.... Why, then, the scene on her love seat the Saturday night before?

"Hmmm. Well, in the meanwhile, he's free. Go after him, Pepper. Have some fun."

Pepper took a deep breath. "I think we should change the subject."

Jenna wasn't quite ready. "Have you done anything . . . beside breakfast?"

"Painted his house. How's your family? Have you spoken with them lately?"

"He hasn't actually asked you out?"

Exasperated, Pepper sighed. "We went to dinner last weekend."

"Great! Did you have fun?"

"Of course I did. I told you. He's a really nice guy."

Jenna stared at Pepper for several long moments. "And you don't want to talk about him."

"There's nothing to talk about, Jenna. Really. He's just . . . a guy."

When Jenna grinned, it was with a hint of smugness. In the months she'd known Pepper, she'd never seen her as defensive. "If you say so." Tossing her long hair back over her shoulder, she acceded to Pepper's earlier question. "Okay. My family. They're fine. I talked with my sister last week and got all the dirt. She wants me to come down for Labor Day."

"Labor Day!" Pepper made a face. "It seems like summer's just begun. I haven't thought that far ahead."

"Neither had I, but Julie sure has. Not that I should be surprised. She always was the organizer. This year's event is to be a family reunion on Hilton Head."

"Oh, Jenna, that sounds like fun!"

"To you, maybe. You don't know my brothers and sisters. They're so . . . successful . . . it could make you sick!"

"You're successful, too. And they are your brothers and sisters. You haven't seen them since . . . well, certainly since before I met you. Aren't you anxious to see your parents?"

"Not if they start in about my life-style. They've never been able to accept the fact that I choose to live in a quiet little town and paint to my heart's content, that there are more important things to me than the latest model Oldsmobile or an invitation to the Birchalls' ball. I've always been the black sheep; we argue whenever we see one another. With things going so well now, I'm not sure I want the hassle."

"But that's just it. Things are going well for you. Wouldn't you like to show them how well? I'd think there'd be a lot of satisfaction in it for you. You know—pick up a new outfit or two, some new shoes. Show them you can play their game. . . ."

Jenna speared an olive that looked lonely in her otherwise empty salad plate and ate it with gusto. "Now that you mention it, that's not such a bad idea. Of course, it verges on the hypocritical—"

"Who cares? The important thing is that you see your family. If they think the worst of you now, you've got nowhere to go but up."

Jenna chuckled. "That's convoluted logic, since I don't really care what they think of me."

"I don't believe that for a minute," Pepper rejoined softly. "I'd think it would be impossible for a person to have family like that and . . . not care."

"Whoa, now. Look who's talking. Weren't you the one who told me that you hadn't seen your father in years?"

"That's different. I was very young when he left. I don't have the . . . memories you have."

"Do you ever wonder about him?"

Pepper drew a faint line on the tablecloth with her fingernail. "Sometimes. More so lately."

"Why, do you think?"

"I suppose because I'm getting older. I look around and see friends who are parents themselves, and I compare their situation to what I had."

"Is it painful?" Jenna asked softly. It wasn't often that the vulnerable side of Pepper showed; her eyes looked suddenly older, sadder.

"No. Well, yes, maybe, in a remote kind of way. When my parents first separated, the pain was unbelievable. As the years passed, it faded. Now it comes from time to time in the form of 'what ifs.'" She smiled sheepishly.

"You know, what if he'd never left, what if she hadn't died, what if I'd grown up in a big, noisy, fun-filled house—"

"We can all imagine the ideal, Pep. I'm not sure it ever really exists."

"You came pretty close," Pepper reminded her, snapping back to her usual perkiness with a speed that caught Jenna off guard. "You've told me stories of your childhood that make it sound pretty fine, even in spite of your so-called black sheep status. Come on. Admit it. Your family's not all that bad."

What Jenna was prepared to admit first off was that she had, indeed, told Pepper any number of stories of her childhood. Pepper seemed to thrive on them, as though some small part of her lived vicariously through the anecdotes.

"All right. I admit it. My family's not all that bad. Hey, why don't you come to Hilton Head with me and meet them?"

"Oh, Jenna, I couldn't—"

"Why not?" She was warming to the idea by the minute. "It'd be fun. Do you have other plans for Labor Day?"

"Labor Day's still more than six weeks off! I told you before, I haven't begun to think—"

"Then begin now. It'd be great. If I had an ally I could really operate from a position of strength."

Pepper laughed. "You're beginning to sound like a corporate shark. I think you're more like your family than you realize," she suggested, then deftly caught the waiter's eye and signaled for the bill. To her relief, Jenna saw an acquaintance at a table across the room and went to say hello. By the time she'd returned, the subject of visiting her family was forgotten.

Pepper thought of it that night, though. Jenna had dropped her back at her place shortly before nine. Alone, she wandered from the loft to the living room, then up again, opening every window as wide as she could, wondering where the breeze was. Finally, stripping off every piece of clothing she wore, she stretched full length on top of the bed, threw an arm over her eyes and sighed.

She couldn't go to Hilton Head with Jenna. It would be too hard. Did a blind man go to a fireworks display, or a deaf one to a symphony? There was no point in reminding herself of all that she didn't have. There was no point in dwelling on it.

Abruptly jumping up, she tugged on a loose, sleeveless nightshirt and ran down to put on a record. Music soothed her. She stretched out flat on the cool wooden floor and tried to concentrate on the melody. But its magic eluded her. She felt strangely restless.

Pushing herself to her feet, she went to the refrigerator and poured herself a glass of lemonade. She sat on the love seat and drank it, then returned to the loft to pick up the book she'd started several nights before. It was a bestseller, newly published in paperback. Rick had raved about it, as had Pam. For the life of her, she couldn't get into it.

The record ended. Padding downstairs, she replaced it in its jacket and returned it to its slot on the shelf.

Switching off the lights, she retreated to the loft, where she turned onto her side in bed and stared out at the beech tree beyond her window.

John's image came to mind; she doggedly pushed it away, only to find it back moments later. With it came remembrance of the way he'd kissed her, touched her, caressed her. She wondered what it would be like to be with him, wondered if it would be as satisfying as the books said.

When she finally fell asleep, it was with a feeling of loneliness the likes of which she hadn't known for years.

PEPPER AWOKE EARLY Sunday morning feeling strangely lethargic. She hadn't slept well and wasn't sure why. Rolling out of bed, she made a cup of coffee, then sat on a tall stool at the counter, chin in hands, wondering what to do with her day. She could clean or do laundry. Maybe take a drive to the beach . . . But alone?

She straightened. She always went places alone. What was wrong with her?

She was about to soothe herself in a long jasmine bath when the phone rang. She frowned. It was eight o'clock. "Hello?"

"Pepper?" came a slightly unsure voice.

She'd recognize it regardless of what tone it took. "John! Hello!"

"I . . . didn't wake you, did I?"

"A morning person like me?" She laughed, feeling suddenly better. "No, you didn't wake me. I was just trying to decide what to do with myself. Somehow I can't get excited at the thought of cleaning. Or doing laundry. Or working in the yard." She tried to help out there whenever she could; it was the least she could do in thanks for the lovely apartment she had.

"How about the beach? Can you get excited about that?"

He'd read her mind. She grinned. "I think I can."

"I'll pick you up in an hour?"

"I'll be ready."

When she hung up the phone, she made a delighted jump in the air. Then, cautioning herself to act her age, she headed for her bath.

5

DRIVING SOUTH past Portland, they arrived at the beach to find that half the population of Maine had had the same idea.

"I didn't realize it'd be so crowded," Pepper commented, helping John remove towels and a cooler from the back of the Scout.

"No problem. If you don't mind a little walk, I'm sure we can find a place for ourselves."

Arms laden they did just that, dropping their things on a patch of sand that was the slightest bit removed from the worst of the crowd. John spread an oversized beach towel on the sand, then whipped his T-shirt over his head, dropped it by the cooler and reached for the snap of his cutoffs.

Pepper busied herself with her own clothes, vividly aware of each bit of skin being bared as he stripped. Without a second thought that morning she'd put on her bikini beneath her own shorts and shirt; suddenly she wished she'd worn something less revealing. But she didn't have anything less revealing, she reminded herself. It had never been an issue before. And it shouldn't be now.

Undressing without further pause, she stretched out on the towel and closed her eyes to the sun. "Ahhh, this feels good."

"Want some lotion?" came the deep voice beside her.

"Not yet. Maybe a little later when I begin to feel the heat."

John was already feeling the heat. He may have seen Pepper barebreasted, but nothing quite prepared him for the way she looked in a bikini. Her skin was butter smooth and golden, her breasts pert, her stomach flat. He could see the hint of white low on her abdomen where the bathing suit must have lain on earlier outings. It was all he could do not to touch her there; using the utmost control, he lay down on his stomach beside her.

"You've got a nice tan," he said softly. "Been here before?"

"Not to this beach," she replied, careful to keep her eyes closed. "There were several warm weekends in June when I hit other ones. There's something about the sound of people laughing, the rhythm of the waves hitting the shore...." There was also something about the excitement of being with John; she was determined to enjoy every minute of it.

When he remained silent, she tipped her head to the side and stole a glance at him through slitted lashes. His face was toward her, his eyes closed. She noted the way his hair was mussed, the way the sea breeze ruffled it even more. Her gaze slid down. His shoulders were strong, sinewed, tapering along his torso to a waist that was lean. He wore a dark blue suit that, while a sight more decent than the skimpy nylon ones some men wore, clung to his firm buttocks in a way that stirred her pulse. His legs were long and spattered with light hair. She suddenly ached to touch them and, by way of prevention, tucked her hands beneath her hips.

She raised her eyes to find John's waiting. "Everything okay?" he asked with a hint of amusement.

"Yeah," she drawled. "You look great."

"So do you. I like your suit. You've got the figure for it."

She pressed her eyes shut and faced the sun once again. "Thank you." But her eyes flew back open when a warm hand touched her stomach.

"Shhh," he murmured. "It's okay. I couldn't resist. Your skin is so soft." Her skin might have been soft, but at that moment her muscles were like a rock. Every one of her senses was alert to the feel of his hand on her flesh.

"Wouldn't it be great," she managed, mildly hoarse, "if I came away from the day with a pale hand mark in the middle of my stomach?"

Chuckling, he removed his hand. "I get the message. Not that I'd mind it. Touch me whenever you get the urge," he invited, then flipped his head to the other side and shifted the sand more comfortably beneath him.

Pepper had the urge, and since he'd offered. . . . Rolling to her side, propping herself on an elbow, she ran her palm across the corded swells of his shoulders.

"Mmm, that feels good," he murmured.

Sitting up cross-legged, she used both hands to massage his back. His flesh was firm and warm, a joy to touch. "You've got a beauty mark," she observed, touching the deep brown spot with her fingertip.

He shivered. "I know. There's another one on the back of my thigh."

She looked down, then turned to explore it. While she was there, she did as she'd ached to do moments before and let her fingers coast down his legs to ruffle the gleaming hairs with delight before returning. Feeling bolder than she ever had, she touched the skin just beneath where his trunks ended.

"It's paler here. Your cutoffs are too long."

"Any shorter," he said in a muffled voice, "and they'd really set the town on its ear. Please, let's observe some propriety."

Pepper jerked her hands away. "I'm sorry." She lay down on her stomach, palms piggy-backed beneath her chin. "You're right." She cleared her throat. "Propriety."

John's grin was in full force when he turned his head her way. "I was referring to Naples. This beach is another matter."

"This beach is *worse*. There are people all over the place." Indeed, even in the few minutes they'd been lying on the sand, their territory had been invaded. Two young couples, very obviously high on the bright sun and each other, had dropped their things nearby before running, amid gay laughter, toward the water. "Ahhh, the joys of youth," she quipped philosophically.

"They can't be much younger than you are." At times he still felt like an old man next to Pepper; she seemed so young, so spirited, so . . . untamed.

"They are. Take my word for it."

"How could you tell?"

"The girls were giggling. I don't giggle."

"Ahhh." John nodded, doing his best to stifle the urge to laugh aloud. "The embodiment of maturity."

She grinned. "I didn't say *that*."

"You're in a good mood."

Their faces were inches apart. Pepper felt his silvery gaze melt into hers. "Of course. It's a beautiful, carefree Sunday."

"What did you do last night?" he asked, throwing caution to the winds.

"Went out for dinner."

"Oh."

"With my friend Jenna," Pepper said after a meaningful pause. It was her turn to be amused; John was positively adorable—and transparent—when he was jealous. "She's an artist with a studio in town. She's a real character."

"So the two of you went out for dinner?"

"Mmm. We hadn't had a chance to visit in a while."

"Did you . . . visit?"

"Uh-huh. How about you? What did you do last night?"

"Slept."

"With whom?"

In answer, he swatted her over the head. "You've got a fresh mouth. You know that?"

"So I've been told on occasion."

"It's also very tempting. . . ." His gaze focused on her lips. She licked them provocatively and was satisfied when he moaned. "I'm not sure this was such a hot idea after all."

"It's hot."

"That's the trouble. . . . Come on." He pushed himself up and grabbed for her hand. "Let's take a swim."

Moments later, they were dodging the waves. When they reached a point deep enough, John released her hand and dived. Pepper followed the graceful arc of his body with hungry eyes, then dived in after him stroking for all she was worth until she reached the point where he'd finally stopped and was treading water.

"It's cold!" she exclaimed, submerging quickly and resurfacing with her head back so that her hair was out of her eyes.

"That was the point!" he growled, reaching out and tugging her forward.

"We'll drown . . ." she began as his arms went around her. Her own settled quite naturally around his neck.

"No, we won't. I've got you."

"But who's got *you?*" she argued, even though she felt the gentle motion of his legs holding them both up as the surf drew them forward, then backward in lilting rhythm.

"You do," he murmured, sliding his arms down past her hips to take her legs and wrap them around him. "This is how I want you." He pressed her closer. His body elaborated on its own.

"Hmm, so much for cold water."

"When you're that hot. . . ." He never finished what he'd started to say, for his lips found hers and devoured them as the next wave sucked them under.

Pepper couldn't believe how aroused she was herself. Hands clutching the back of John's head while their lips clung, she floated higher against him. When they re-emerged from the wave, he propelled them farther in until his feet touched the mobile ocean floor.

"You feel right in my arms," he murmured, "right against me all the way." He kissed her again, hands cupping her bottom, rubbing her more firmly against him.

She gasped for air when he finally released her mouth and buried her face in his neck. The water lapped at his shoulders, rising and falling in mime of her hips beneath his touch. "Oh, John," she whispered, clearly identifying the need she felt as the same that had nagged at her the night before.

"Like that?"

"Oh, yes."

He slipped a hand into her bikini bottom and held her soft flesh as he continued to ever-gently knead her against his hardness. "I've thought about you so much since last weekend."

"You've seen me almost every day—"

"Not this way. God, you're driving me crazy. If we were in a more private place . . ."

Her insides quivered madly. "What . . . ?"

"I'd. . . ."

"Go on."

He lowered his mouth to her earlobe and sucked on it before speaking. "You want me to tell you?"

"Yes," she whispered, driven by a demon that seemed to suddenly possess her. She'd never in her life played games like this and might have been frightened had they indeed been in a more private place. But they weren't. There were people on the beach, frolicking in the water not far from them.

He spoke softly into her ear. "If we were in a more private place, I'd take off this bra to feel your breasts against me." He paused, breathing raggedly.

"Then...?"

He squeezed the flesh of her bottom in a way that heralded his words. "Then I'd slip this bit of nothing down over your legs and touch you."

When his fingers slid lower, deeper, she made a soft, whimpering sound. Coiled around his shoulders, her arms trembled.

"Should I go on?"

She squeezed her eyes shut, aware of the tantalizing motion of his fingers and what it was doing to her. She was intoxicated. "Yes," she whispered in a gasp.

"Then I'd hold you off only long enough to get rid of my trunks. When I brought you back to me, I'd wrap your legs around my waist just where they are now...."

She held her breath. "And...?"

"And I'd be inside you, Pepper. Deep inside you." His hips simulated the act with a firm thrust that drove his fingers all the more intimately into her waiting warmth.

Pepper's heart beat furiously within the breast that was flattened against him. A knot of desire tightened at the point where his fingers delved, and a soft sound of need slipped from her throat. "Oh, John," she whispered, suddenly wanting everything he'd described and more.

He released her only to take her face in his hands. "I want you, sweetheart. Would you let me do that to you . . . those things I said? Would you let me inside?"

His urgency brought reality back with the next wave. Slowly, she released his waist and let her legs slide down to bob against his. But his hands tightened in response; he wasn't about to let her go without an answer.

"Maybe."

There was nothing coy in her softly spoken word; he sensed she was waging a tiny war within. So far, it appeared his tactics were right on the money. It was getting harder for him to hold back—it had been pure hell not asking her to spend the entire weekend with him—but if it paid off in the end. . . .

He walked them in a little farther until she too could stand. "Is that a maybe as in when I get to know you better?"

Eyes round, she nodded. She looked so open, so vulnerable, so desirable, then he took her in his arms a final time and gave her a tight squeeze. "Then I guess I'll have to wait. Besides—" he released her and grinned "—it wouldn't do to make a scene here. The tide would have a heyday with our suits. I can just see us diving barebottomed in search of them."

She couldn't help but laugh at the picture he painted. Her limbs still trembled from his throaty suggestions, but she took several deep breaths and managed to restore her calm. She knew what she was doing—she'd been in control, hadn't she? *Hadn't she?*

She was still wondering about that when John dived backward, swimming vigorously away from shore before returning. Understanding that he needed the time and exertion to control the urge he'd been unable to hide even at the end, she smiled and dived in herself, stroking calmly, then rolling onto her back and letting the force of the surf sweep her toward shore.

She was already stretched out on the towel when John returned, and she looked up only to give him a reassuring smile. He was slightly winded; she could hear his lingering gasps when he lowered himself to lie by her side.

"Everything okay?" she asked when his breathing had grown more steady.

"Yup." He reached over, threading his fingers through her hair and twisting it gently to one shoulder. "I'm a patient man. I can wait."

It sounded as much like a self-directive as a simple reply to her question. In either case, she was satisfied. It had occurred to her that he might start to push; a lesser man would call her a tease for what had happened...twice now. John seemed to understand, though, and she was grateful. If she was teasing, it was neither intentional nor malicious. It was all so new to her, this intense sexual something she felt for him. Too much, too fast, might spoil it all.

Fortunately, she was enough of a realist to know that the attraction wouldn't simply die with her plea—and his agreement—for restraint. If anything, it grew as the day progressed, fed by physical closeness, even by such innocent things as cold fried chicken passed back and forth between them and shared drinks. They swam and sunbathed, and Pepper was reminded that the attraction she felt for him was far deeper than physical. He was a delight to be with even when he scolded her for getting sand in the soda. She felt strangely full inside—even without the soft-murmured promise he'd made—and an odd pride at being there by his side. Only an occasional thought was spared for the lavender lady, but it was thrust aside with the reminder of Jenna's words. The lavender lady wasn't there, was she? Tough luck, lavender lady.

By four in the afternoon, they'd gathered their things and headed back to the Scout. By unspoken consent, once the seats had cooled enough for them to sit without yelping, they took a leisurely drive along the coastal roads.

"It's so pretty around here," Pepper mused. "This is what I love about New England. One minute you can be in the country, surrounded by trees and grass and the silence of the earth, the next you can be at the shore, entranced by the ocean."

"I know." John had pulled the Scout onto the shoulder of the road overlooking the surf. "You're very much at ease with the water. Did you spend much time at the beach as a child?"

"Some," she said, vaguely recollecting an occasional outing when her parents had still been together. She wished she'd been older then; the memories would have been stronger. "I always took to the water, even if it was a rubber pool in the backyard or a long bath, for that matter. I didn't really learn to swim till I was a little older. My mother's cousins loved the shore; as long as I occupied myself there, they were happy. I spent most of my time in the water then. It was mutually satisfying all around."

"Were they ogres?"

"Nah. They were okay. Just stuck with a situation they hadn't asked for."

"What about your father? Didn't he try to contact you after your mother died?"

She shook her head, then wrinkled her nose in a gesture of nonchalance that didn't quite make it. Her voice held the note of sadness she'd tried to deny. "I assume he had his own life. He may have remarried. For all I know I've got a slew of half brothers and sisters."

"Do you ever get the urge to try and find him?"

"For what purpose? I've got my own life. I don't need him."

John didn't quite believe that, but he made no further comment. It had occurred to him, in the long hours he'd spent contemplating Pepper and her past, that she very much needed some contact with her father. Much as she tried to minimize any continuing hurt, he sensed its presence. He'd also begun to think more about her single status and wondered if it had very much to do with that past. Perhaps if she saw her father, talked with him, aired the anger and hurt she'd harbored all these years.... But that was the counselor at work, and the counselor in John said that, whatever happened, Pepper had to want to do it. He could only suggest, then hope. As for the man in him, well, he prayed it wouldn't take too long.

He started the Scout again and they drove farther, stopping for lobsters at a takeout place and eating them on the rocks overlooking the sea. Their conversation was lighter; he made no reference to her father again. Even the silence between them was companionable. Stretched out on the rocks, their bellies filled, there seemed no better way to end the day.

That was before they were heading back to Naples and John spotted a drive-in movie. "Wow! I didn't think these things still existed!" He pulled into the nearest driveway and executed a deft U-turn.

"John! Drive-ins are for kids!"

But his eyes were glued to the huge signpost they approached. "Look! *Creature from the Black Lagoon!* Come on, Pepper. Let's!"

"John—"

"Have you seen it? No, you haven't." He was pulling into line before the entrance. "This is great! I haven't been to a drive-in in years!" He might have rubbed his hands together had they not been preoccupied with the wheel.

"I don't like horror movies."

"That's okay. This one's not all that scary. Besides, I'll be here. You can just hold my hand and close your eyes at the bad parts."

"And when I have nightmares tonight?"

"You can . . . you can call me on the phone and I'll be over in a flash."

"I'm sure."

"I will!"

"I'm sure."

"Oh." He inched the Scout forward. "No, it's not what you think. I promise I won't take advantage of you. But think, Pep. *Creature from the Black Lagoon* is a classic!"

"It's on TV every other month."

"I don't own a TV. Would you deny me this one small treat?"

His enthusiasm was neither to be believed nor dampened. His face glowed in a boyish way, entreating her. How could she refuse?

Taking a deep breath, she let it out in a whoosh. "All right. But I'll have you know that I'm doing this just for you. And if I get sick all over your car when some atrocious monster starts mutilating helpless victims—"

John snagged her neck with his arm and dragged her closer, smacking her forehead with a kiss. "That's my girl! I knew I could count on you!" He stepped hard on the brake when the Scout came within inches of the car ahead, but released Pepper only when they'd approached the ticket window and he had to dig for his wallet.

Moments later they were parked at the back of the large drive-in theater. "The screen's big enough," John explained, hooking the speaker onto his window. "We're higher than most of the cars. If we move closer, they won't be able to see over us."

Pepper snickered. "You can move back a few rows if you'd like." Then they'd be out of the theater altogether.

John gave her a knowing smile. "This will do, I believe. Be grateful we don't have to wear 3-D glasses; this must be a modification of the original movie."

"Lovely."

Ignoring her sarcasm, he did rub his hands together then. "So. How about some popcorn? Candy? Soda?"

"Sure. What the hell. Might as well do it right."

"Which'll it be?"

"All three."

"All three." He paused. "Right. Be back in a minute."

Pepper watched him bound from the Scout and jog to the refreshment stand not far away. It had been a long time since she'd been to a drive-in, too. The last time she'd spent the night fighting off one Harlan Frisch. But John would be different. He understood her hesitance. Besides, he was so excited about seeing *Creature from the Black Lagoon* that she doubted he'd even remember her existence once the movie began.

In actuality, their hands were busied with popcorn and drinks when the film started. "This is great!" John said as the story of the anthropologists in search of the merman began to unfold.

"Shhh. I'm trying to listen," Pepper scolded between mouthfuls of popcorn. She was also trying not to imagine the snakes and crocodiles that would be swarming all over the Amazon basin.

When the music rose to suggest that the creature might appear, she averted her eyes and saw that John was clearly mesmerized by the drama. She couldn't be angry; he was enjoying himself so.

"Look! There it is!"

"Oh, yuk." She reached for the soda and took a long drink, then popped a Milk Dud into her mouth and chewed it. "Is it gone?"

"Back in the swamp."

Breathing more freely, she raised her eyes to the screen. It wasn't bad, she decided, though she wished it was in color rather than black and white. A short while later, though, when she was taken off guard and found herself eye to eye with the creature, she was grateful indeed that the film wasn't in color.

She sucked in a breath and stared, disgusted, as the thing on the screen tried to cope with the invasion of its territory. Groaning, she looked away. John put his arm around her and hauled her closer to his side.

"Did you see that fish face?"

"It was vile."

"And the scales." He laughed gleefully. "I love the expressions when the creature appears. Now, those people were actors."

"Hmmph. Doesn't take much acting to be put off by the sight of something like that—"

"But look at the woman. There. See? She's fascinated."

"*She's* the only actor in the bunch."

John gave her shoulder a squeeze. "Come on, sweetheart. Where's your imagination?"

"Oh, it's there. Believe me, it's there."

Settling back into the crook of his shoulder, she helped herself to another Milk Dud, then held one up for John. He took it, nipping her finger with his teeth.

"Ahh! Be careful!"

"My gosh, was that you?" Momentarily forgetting the creature, he studied her finger in the dark, then took it in his mouth and sucked on it. Pepper had to admit that his tongue had an instantly soothing effect. "Better?" he asked softly.

"Better."

They both returned their eyes to the screen, but Pepper, for one, was more conscious of John's thigh beneath her hand than she was of the creature's growing fascination with the anthropologist's beautiful assistant. She wasn't sure how her hand had come to be there, simply knew that it felt very comfortable. Her fingers lay relaxed against his firm muscle; she experimented, inching them to the side to more fully appreciate the fine texture of his skin.

His hand closed over hers and stilled its small movement. She looked back at the screen. The anthropologists were trying to decide how to handle the creature; the bad guy wanted to kill it, the good guy did not. Dry, she thought. Really dry. She tipped her head back to see that John's eyes were glued to the screen. On impulse, she placed a warm kiss on his jaw.

His eyes never left the screen. The hand that had circled her shoulder slipped up to settle her head against his neck. Pepper tried to watch the movie from that vantage point, but the steady beat of his pulse distracted her. It was soft; she felt it more than heard it. And he smelled good, a blend of sea salt and man, very earthy, decidedly appealing.

Nestling sideways, she slipped an arm around his waist and closed her eyes. She was tired in a satisfied kind of way. A day at the beach could do that to a person. She rubbed her cheek against the fabric of his T-shirt, liking the fact that it was just thin enough to allow for the tiniest feel through of the crisp hairs on his chest. Abandoning his waist, she rested her hand on his heart. Now *that* was a heartbeat!

"Pepper," John asked softly, "what are you doing?"

"Just resting."

"Are you bored?"

"No. Just . . . resting."

He paused. "Okay." Shifting slightly on his seat, he draped his arm around her back. His hand rested on her ribs.

The crescendo of the music was ample excuse for Pepper's not looking at the screen. Something terrible was about to happen, and she didn't care to watch. Instead, she began to trace small circles with her palm on John's chest. She measured the firm upper swell in a slow, creeping motion, stole lower to explore his ribs, then rose again to find her palm covering the hard nub of his nipple.

"Pepper . . ." Just a hint of warning.

"Sorry." She stilled her hand immediately and waited, moving only to brush the back of her knee against the upholstered seat. It occurred to her that John was working harder at breathing, but she wasn't sure whether she or the film was at fault. Somehow she saw a challenge there. It wouldn't do for her ego to think that the creature could do things to him that she couldn't.

Curling her fingers into her palm, she moved the fist—with agonizing slowness—down the center of his chest, trailing with her thumb, which dipped into his navel before coming to a halt where his cutoffs began.

When John grabbed her hand and pressed it to the erection she'd evoked, she had her answer. Then, before she could catch her breath from the blatant evidence of her success, he thrust his fingers in her hair, tipped her head back and took her lips in a kiss more powerful, more dizzying, more masterful than anything that had come before. His mouth surged hungrily over hers, slanting and sucking, applying just enough pressure and varying it accordingly, to send her senses whirling.

"You're a minx," he growled before renewing the kiss in an even more persuasive manner. Even after a day at the beach, the faintest hint of jasmine clung to her skin. Neither the smell of popcorn nor the more musty scent of the drive-in itself could overpower it. It was driving him mad.

Light-headed, Pepper returned his passion, her tongue seeking with greater boldness all that it had missed before. When he touched her breasts, she caught her breath, then opened her mouth wider as a bursting pleasure drove her on. Her nipples hardened; he found them, rolled them, tugged them until she clutched his shoulder and strained closer. When he slid his hand lower, she couldn't protest, for the emptiness was back, deep inside her, needing assuagement.

"So much better...than the movie...." she whispered in broken gasps.

"I think I...agree." Deftly unsnapping her shorts, he tugged down the zipper and slipped his hand inside before she realized what he'd done. Then it was too late, for his fingers had broached the final barrier and found the soft curls at the apex of her thighs.

On pure reflex, she pressed her knees together, but they were trembling and she couldn't think straight with his tongue stroking the inside of her mouth the way it was. His fingers worked gently, caressing her in tiny circles while the hand around her back stole beneath her T-shirt, then her bikini bra, to close over her hot flesh. She moaned into his mouth.

"Relax, sweetheart," he whispered back. "Open your legs...."

His words sent an electric ripple through her veins. She wanted to deny him, wanted to tell herself—and him—to stop, but she couldn't. What he was doing to her felt too good. She didn't have the willpower to resist it or the promise of pleasure that beckoned.

Slowly, enraptured, she let her knees fall apart.

"That's it." His breath was a husky murmur at the corner of her mouth. The music from the speaker increased in tempo, but neither noticed. "That's it . . . just relax. . . ." Taking her lips again, he slipped his fingers lower, deeper. In his other hand, her nipple was pebble hard, responding to his skillful manipulation.

"John? I don't. . . ."

"Shhh. It's okay. Let me. . . ."

He was stroking her deeply, touching where no man had touched before save that very morning, when his motions had been cushioned by the sea. Now there was nothing to dilute the eruption of sensation. Taking shallow little breaths, Pepper tried to understand what she was feeling, but there was only a burning, a greater need, a pleasure so intense that she could do nothing but barrel forward, headlong toward this mysterious source of delight.

She was losing control. She knew it, but she was helpless to fight. Suddenly her body grew tense, striving, aching, dangling on the precipice of something new and alive.

She whimpered softly. "John . . . John?"

His voice was a velvet murmur by her ear. "That's it, sweetheart. Let it come."

"I don't . . . know. . . ."

Increasing the pressure, he slid a finger deeper. It was all she needed. With the marginal penetration, she stiffened, then exploded into a million brilliant sparks all radiating from her core to cause spasm after spasm of blinding joy.

The next thing she knew, she was gasping for breath while John eased her back from the heaven where she'd been. Slowly he withdrew his hand and slid his arms around her to give her a gentle hug. He only spoke when he sensed she could hear him once more, and then it was with a satisfied smile on his face.

"How was that?"

"Oh, John . . ." She buried her face against his chest. "What did . . . you do?"

"I pleasured you, just as I've been wanting to do all day."

"I've never . . . that's never . . . happened. . . ."

He held her back, brushing damp wisps of hair from her cheeks. "You've never felt that?" When she shook her head, eyes soulful, he realized anew how precious she was. Bringing her against him again, he gently rubbed her back. "Then you've been with all the wrong men. And I'm glad I was the first."

Feeling lethargic enough not to correct his misconception, Pepper lay against him. She wasn't that naive; she did know, technically, what had happened. Emotionally, well, she wouldn't dwell on it. It had happened; she had enjoyed it. And she, too, was glad that John had been the first.

With his heart beating steadily by her ear, she soon fell asleep, awakening only when a long finger touched her cheek.

"Pepper? The movie's over."

She sat up quickly. "It is?"

"Mmm. You slept through the best part. The creature fell in love with the anthropologist's assistant and tried to steal her away to his cavern at the bottom of the lagoon."

"Was he successful?"

"Now, if I tell you that," John drawled, "I'll spoil it for you another time."

"What other time? Once was enough, thank you."

But he only smiled, then started the Scout, thinking how very innocent Pepper MacNeil truly was.

DETERMINED NOT TO push his luck, John left Pepper at her door that night with a tender kiss, refusing her invitation to come in when he sensed a faint unsureness in her. He was convinced that she needed time to come to terms with the full nature of their relationship. When he'd called her that morning, and asked her to the beach, he'd never dreamed he'd do what, in fact, he'd done. But she'd been so provocative—whether intentionally or not—that he'd been unable to help himself.

Though he knew that she wanted him, he also knew that he wanted her to want him much more before they went further. His own restraint continued to amaze him. Never before had he been willing to wait when he'd felt the kind of desire for a woman that he felt for Pepper. No. He amended that. He'd never before felt quite the same kind of attraction. Having sex with Pepper wasn't good enough; it would be making love . . . or nothing.

6

THE NEXT FEW WEEKS flew by for Pepper. Happier than she'd ever been, she was perfectly content to ignore the tiny voice in her that whispered from time to time of danger. What did *it* know, she reasoned. *She* was the one who saw John every day and she knew what she was doing. He was a good friend; they talked of anything and everything that came to mind. He was also inspirational, showing her a side of her nature that she'd never been able to accept before. She was discovering what a beautiful thing passion was, although there were times when she thought she'd die of wanting more. When John touched her, kissed her—when she stopped to talk with him along her mail route or during the free days she inevitably spent with him—she blossomed. He was a subtle, patient teacher and she adored him for it.

"I think you're in love with the man," Pam stated one Sunday morning in early August when she'd dropped by unannounced on the chance that Pepper might be free for once. They were sitting in the shade of the large beech tree beside Pepper's garage.

"You're nuts."

"Am I? You seem to spend every minute you can with him. You said it yourself—if it weren't for the fact that right now he's at a brunch with some of the school administrators, you'd be over there staining his wood-work."

"That's got nothing to do with love. I *like* him. He's a *friend*."

"Uh-huh."

"He is."

"You're deluding yourself, Pep."

"No, I'm not. My eyes are wide open. I know exactly what I'm doing. I have no intention of falling in love. I'd only be hurt."

"What makes you so sure?"

"How can you even ask that, Pam?" Pepper returned with uncharacteristic impatience. "You've been married and divorced. Weren't you hurt?"

Leaning back against the smooth bark of the beech, Pam eyed her friend with mild amusement. "Not particularly." When Pepper simply stared, she explained. "Joel and I weren't really in love. I discovered that very quickly when we ran into problems. His mother may have been the catalyst, but there wasn't much to try to save. We'd been young and more in love with the idea of love than with each other. The divorce was a relief."

Pepper pondered that for a moment. "Would you ever think to try again?"

"I'd love to."

"How could you be sure that the same thing wouldn't happen a second time?"

"I'm older, for one thing. And wiser, as the saying goes. I know what I want and what I don't want. Unfortunately," she drawled, "we're talking hypothetical here.

Knowing what I want is one thing, finding it another. Maybe if your John Smith wasn't so taken with you, he'd give someone else a chance."

"He's not *taken* with me," Pepper mocked, but she knew he was. Or rather, she knew that he was seeing no one else and that there'd been neither mention of, nor mail from, the lavender lady in weeks. "We're just...just...."

"Yes?" Pam prodded, a smug smile on her face.

"Compatible." Pepper grinned. "I'm a joy to be with. You know that."

"Ah, yes."

"You'll see. When school starts in the fall, John won't have time for me," she stated, burying a hint of anxiety in characteristic flippancy. "The house will be done, he'll have friends from New York up on weekends, it'll be different."

"I wouldn't be so sure of that, Pepper, my friend. I wouldn't be so sure of it at all."

Fall—and school—were still a month off on the day that John begged Pepper to help him wallpaper the bathrooms. Addicted as she'd become to his company, she couldn't refuse him.

"This is going to be interesting," she remarked, opening one of the rolls of paper and studying its bold pattern. "You did have to choose geometrics—"

"Now just a minute, sweetheart. We went shopping together. *You* were the one who said you loved geometrics."

"That was before I realized I'd have to help hang them," she returned, then caught herself. "Don't you like them?"

"Of course I like them." He smiled, kissing away the furrows on her brow. "I probably would have chosen them even if you *hadn't* liked them. It just makes it nicer that you do. Anyway—" he straightened and turned to study the bathroom walls "—you got the better end of the deal. *You* didn't have to steam the old stuff off and then repair all the ugly little cracks in the wall." Resting his hands on his hips, he scowled. "There are times when I wonder just what I'll find next. I swear, there are more things in need of repair—"

Pepper's fingers on his lips silenced his complaint. "You're doing a beautiful job, John," she said softly. "Have I told you that? Every day I see new things you've done, and then when I stand back and remember what it was like when you first showed me around, I'm in awe. You should be very proud of yourself. Really. When you're done, this place will be a masterpiece."

His expression softened to one she didn't dare categorize. "You're very good for me, Pepper. Thank you."

Changing gears with customary deftness, she nudged him in the ribs and refocused on the walls. "Don't thank me so fast. When you've got wallpaper hanging lopsided from the ceiling, curling around the mirror, dragging in the toilet—"

He stilled her with a kiss, after which she quickly turned to the wallpaper. They started with the smallest of the three bathrooms upstairs on the theory that mistakes there would be least likely to be seen. Working well as a team, they managed to match up lines and patterns so that when they'd finished the first room and stopped for lunch, they were both proud as punch.

The afternoon's work was more trying. For one thing, the particular pattern John had chosen for the second upstairs bathroom was a more complex one. For another, the walls seemed to be much more broken up by mirrors and windows and light switches. It was nearly four when, backs aching, they finally gave up for the day.

"Let me tell you," Pepper teased, "covering my route tomorrow will be a vacation after today." Armed with cans of soda, they'd strolled out to the backyard to collapse beneath the peach tree. Lying flat on her back, Pepper looked up. "You've got a good crop. What are you going to do with them all?"

John plucked two of the more rosy peaches from a low branch and handed her one. "Feed them to lovely ladies who are good enough to spend their days off hanging wallpaper with me." Settling by her side, propped on an elbow, he watched her take a big bite.

"Mmm." She chewed. "Delicious."

Leaning forward, he licked a dot of moisture that lingered on her lips. She shivered.

"Cold?" he asked, grinning.

She sat up, moving several inches away in the process. "You know I'm not. I start to shake every time you do that to me."

"I've never licked peach juice from your mouth before."

"You're right. Let me see." She tapped a finger against her lip. "Once it was strawberry jam." That had been when she'd made breakfast for him at her place the week before. "Another time it was ice cream." Then they'd stopped at a Dairy Queen after renting a sander for the floors. "Either I'm a particularly sloppy eater, or you've got a particularly quirky fixation."

He quirked both brows but didn't nip at her bait. Rather he offered some of his own. "I thought I'd try to get tickets for Tanglewood. Are you interested?"

Her eyes widened and she sat straighter. "Tanglewood? Am I ever!"

"You've been before, haven't you?"

"No! Vassar wasn't all that far away from Lenox, but during fall and winter the orchestra wasn't there. I've heard the Boston Symphony several times, but never in concert at Tanglewood. This is the first summer I've been close enough, and somehow...well...I just haven't thought to get tickets." The fact was that she'd been so preoccupied with John that it simply hadn't mattered. But if he was suggesting they go together....

"Good enough," he said, eminently satisfied. "I'll see what I can do. It's kind of late, but I think I can pull a few strings and wangle us something."

Pepper beamed. "Oh, John, that would be great!" She watched him shape a grin around his peach and take a huge bite. On impulse, she leaned forward, much as he'd done moments before, and licked a drop of juice from the corner of his mouth.

Groaning, he tossed the peach aside and grabbed her shoulders. He nearly choked in his rush to swallow what he'd barely chewed. "That," he said at last, "cannot go unanswered. You're far too much of a tease. Do you know that?"

In response to the playfulness in his eyes, she grinned. "What are you gonna do about it, big boy?" With thoughts of Tanglewood and the handsome prince before her filling her head, she was feeling suddenly giddy.

"I'm going to give you a taste of your own medicine," he growled. Rising to his knees, broad shoulders dwarfing hers, he took her face in his hands and lowered his mouth. His firm lips opened hers to make room for his tongue, which plunged deeply, then receded, then plunged again. It was a peach-moist kiss that made Pepper reel. She was half relieved when John dragged her T-shirt to her armpits and, hands on her breasts, pressed her back to the grass.

Then she screamed and clutched at his shoulders to push him away.

"What—" he began, but she was sitting up and grabbing for her own shoulder, a look of agony on her face.

"Ah! My God!" She rocked back and forth, obviously in pain.

"What is it—"

"I don't know," she gasped. Her face was contorted. "A bee, I think. It hurts. Oh, damn—"

John was behind her in an instant. "Let me see." Pushing the T-shirt higher, he carefully plucked the stinger from her flesh and held it for her inspection. "You were right. It was a bee. Now that it's stung you, it's gonna die for sure."

"It's not dead yet. That thing's still pulsing. Ahhh...." She was reaching for her back, as though rubbing the spot would ease the pain. "You can't believe how much it hurts."

"I can believe." He took her hand. "Come on. Let's go inside. A cold compress will help."

Her T-shirt straightened on its own and she half ran beside him. "So much for a taste of my own medicine," she mumbled. "I think I've learned my lesson."

John said nothing, but led her quickly through the house to the kitchen, where he grabbed a pitcher of ice water from the refrigerator and began soaking the end of a clean dishtowel. Squeezing the excess into the sink, he tugged up the back of Pepper's T-shirt and pressed the cloth to the small red mark left by the stinger. With his free hand he pushed the shirt higher on her neck.

"Let's get this off. It'll be easier."

Between the two of them, they removed the T-shirt. Even wearing a bra, it didn't occur to Pepper to be self-conscious. She was too preoccupied with the pain in her upper back.

"Better?" He pressed the cloth tighter with one hand, while with the other he swept loose strands of her hair from her shoulders. As always when she worked, she'd caught it up in a ponytail, for coolness and convenience. In spite of it, her skin felt clammy.

"A little. I feel hot."

"This'll help."

But it didn't. When the cloth grew tepid, he doused it afresh and reapplied it. By then, she was bending to touch her legs. Large welts had broken out on her skin. She tried to scratch but couldn't seem to find relief.

"What're these?" he asked, fingering small welts on her lower back.

"I don't know." Her voice was weak, her heart pounding in her chest. "This is absurd. It's only a bee sting."

"I'm wondering—"

"I don't feel well, John."

He was in front of her then, studying her flushed face with his hands and his eyes. She seemed to be breathing with a harshness that couldn't possibly have come from hurrying inside.

"Tell me what you feel, sweetheart." His voice was calm, gentle, but her inner palpitations continued.

"I feel hot . . . cold. My throat. It's so tight. Maybe I'm imagining . . . what's the matter with me?"

He was trying to contain his fear, but it was hard when Pepper, usually so strong, was so obviously afraid. "Have you ever been stung before?"

"No," she cried. "At least, not that I can remember."

Tossing the cloth into the sink, he grabbed for her T-shirt and began propelling her toward the garage. "We're going to the hospital. They'll know what to do." When she began to shiver, he tightened his arm around her. "It's okay, sweetheart. Everything's going to be all right."

The nearest hospital was in Bridgton, an eight mile drive that seemed endless to them both. John held her close to his side, murmuring soft words of encouragement while she trembled.

"I . . . hate hospitals," she gasped in a whisper.

"Shhh. Don't talk. Just rest."

"My mother. . .was sick for three. . .months before she died and I had . . . to go there every. . .day."

"Shhh. You're going to be okay. There's a standard procedure for treating this type of thing. We'll be back home in a flash."

"Oh, John . . . I'm sorry for being so . . . much trouble."

"You're not trouble. If I hadn't been so goddamned hungry—"

"It wasn't your. . . fault. I was hungry. . . too."

He stepped on the brake at a red light and swore softly. Then, when there were no other cars at the crossroad, he didn't bother to wait for the green.

"If the police stop you—"

"We'll have an escort. It wouldn't hurt."

Pepper closed her eyes. Along with alternating waves of hot and cold, she experienced senses of loneliness, then reassurance when he held her tighter. By the time they'd reached the hospital and John had pulled up before the Emergency entrance, she was thinking of nothing beyond trying to breathe. It seemed so difficult.

"Can you walk?" he asked, pulling her gently beneath the steering wheel and out of the Scout.

"I think so." But her legs wobbled and before she knew it he'd swept her up into his arms. She felt ill enough not to object.

What she would have done without John, she didn't know. Dizzy, gasping for air, she was only half aware of the words he spoke to the nurse at the desk. The next thing she knew she was lying on an examining table with an oxygen mask covering her nose and mouth. Terrified, she clung to John's hand as though it were a lifeline.

A doctor was there then, joining the nurse in questioning John. Pepper felt the bind of a tight band as her blood pressure was taken, felt the cold disk of a stethoscope against her hot flesh. Then she heard someone ask John if he would wait outside. As frightened by that prospect as by what was happening to her body, she opened her eyes to see him shaking his head. She had time to breathe only the slightest sigh of relief before she felt a sharp jab in her arm.

"It's okay," John whispered, bending low, stroking her forehead. "Just a shot of Adrenalin." He held her hand tightly.

Then, calmly, the doctor began to explain to her what was happening. "You've had a severe reaction to the bee sting. Did you know you were allergic?" She shook her head. "You've never had anything like this before, even when you were a child?"

"I asked her that," John interjected, "and she said she didn't remember anything like it."

Putting the stethoscope to his ears, the doctor listened to her heart for a minute, then signaled to the nurse, who promptly left. "Usually in a case like this there's been a past sting. She may not have been aware of it. It might not have been as bad as this." He turned his attention to Pepper. "Breathe deeply. The oxygen will help while the Adrenalin gets going there. We'll give you another shot in just a few minutes."

Pepper wanted to say how awful she felt, how much she hated being in this place, but she was too weak. Her heart continued to palpitate, its beat reverberating through her entire body.

When the nurse returned, the doctor busied himself near Pepper's hand. "I'm going to get an IV ready, just in case we decide to use it," he explained. His quiet tone didn't reassure Pepper in the least.

Sensing her fear, John brought her free hand to his chest. He ran his fingers up and down her arm, then pressed her knuckles to his mouth. His eyes sought and held hers, speaking silent words of encouragement. It was hard; he was as frightened as she was. But she seemed to be begging for his strength; and he gave her everything he could.

The second shot did the trick. Very gradually her heartbeat slowed, her throat relaxed and her breathing resumed a semblance of normalcy. Pepper saw the relief on John's face and would have felt it herself as well had it not been for the overwhelming fatigue that enveloped her.

They remained in the Emergency Room for several hours. When the doctor finally suggested that Pepper might stay the night, John spoke quickly, reading her mind. "Is there any further danger?"

"No," the doctor answered, removing the IV needle which, mercifully, he hadn't needed. "The worst is definitely over. I'd like her to take an antihistamine for a day or so. She might be more comfortable here."

"I'd like to take her home, if that's okay. She won't be alone. I'll make sure she takes her medicine." When the doctor nodded, John went on. "Now that we know she reacts like this, what do we do?"

"You've got two choices. Either she can keep a kit with Adrenalin near her all the time. Or she can be sensitized gradually. An allergy shot every three weeks or so for the next two years should do it."

"Anything immediate, while we decide?"

"I'll give you the kit, just in case." He carefully removed the oxygen mask from Pepper's face. "If you decide on allergy shots, they should begin immediately. You were very fortunate that you got here as quickly as you did. Reactions as extreme as this can be life-threatening."

John helped Pepper sit up and get dressed, while the doctor went in search of the antihistamine he was prescribing.

"How are you feeling?" He eased the T-shirt down over her head, then helped her put her arms through the holes.

"Tired," she answered. She sounded tired.

"Does the sting itself still hurt?"

"I think my arm hurts worse."

He chuckled and drew her against him, only then allowing himself to realize the potential danger she'd been in. A shudder passed through his body. He buried his face in her hair, breathing in the jasmine scent that seemed to give him strength. He had pulled back and was pressing a gentle kiss to her forehead when the doctor returned with the pills and his card, both of which John promptly pocketed. Moments later, Pepper was in John's arms again, being carried to the Scout.

"I can walk," she protested softly.

"Maybe so, but it'd be a strain. Indulge me. You're light enough."

"I think you just want an excuse to show how strong you are."

"Y'know, it was nice having that oxygen mask over your mouth. I can do without your wisecracks. You may be able to push this whole thing to the back of your mind, but let me tell you, you gave me a good scare."

When he propped her upright on the seat of the Scout, she clung to his shoulders for a minute. "John? Thank you."

"For what?" He nudged her over and slid behind the wheel.

"For being with me. I was scared, too. I don't know what I'd have done if I'd been alone."

He took her in his arms then and hugged her. "You don't have to be alone, Pepper. I'm here."

She knew he was, could feel the tight support of his arms, but she wondered how long it would last. In that instant, she felt a frisson of fear totally different from any she'd experienced earlier. Reaching deep inside, she sought the private strength that had seen her through so many years alone. But it eluded her. And she didn't have the wherewithal to keep looking for it. She was simply too tired.

During the drive back to John's house, she lay weakly against him. When he scooped her into his arms and carried her directly upstairs to his bedroom, she muttered a feeble protest.

"You should take me home. I'm all right—"

"Well, I'm not. And I won't be if I know you're alone."

Dragging back the covers with a free hand, he set her gently on the sheets. "You shouldn't be alone tonight. Not after what that precious body of yours has been through today.... Are you hungry?"

"Just tired."

"Thirsty?"

"Just tired."

Turning, he went to the dresser and extracted a white shirt, soft and freshly laundered. Then he sat her up and began to undress her.

"John—"

"Shhh." He had her T-shirt over her head. "You'll be more comfortable."

"I don't think—"

"Don't think." Unsnapping her bra, he discarded it, then gently helped her into his shirt. "Just keep still and let me do the thinking for a change." Rolling the sleeves to her elbows, he laid her back and reached for the snap of her shorts.

"John—"

"Pepper...."

Hearing the warning in his voice, she shut her mouth and closed her eyes while he tugged the shorts down, then drew the sheet up to cover her. His next words were a whisper by her ear.

"And if you don't think this is the supreme sacrifice, think again. For all the times I've dreamed of having you in my bed, never once was it under these circumstances."

"I'm sorry," she whispered back, turning onto her side to burrow against him. Moments later she was asleep.

When she awoke, the sun was streaming in through the window. She bolted up, only to wince when her body protested the sudden movement. Beside her, John stirred. She looked over to see that he lay on his stomach. As much as she could see of his broad back was bare. Groggily he turned his head her way, then opened his eyes wide and pushed himself up.

"I thought for sure I'd wake up before you did!"

"I have to go to work, John!"

"No, you don't. I called last night. Will is taking over for you today."

"You . . . called? John, you had no right—"

"How do you feel?"

"Okay."

"How do you really feel?"

"I'm fine!" Turning away from him, she slid her legs to the floor and started to stand, only to stop midway and sink back to the bed. "My legs feel like soggy rubber," she said in a leaden voice, then pressed her face into her hands.

John was behind her, dragging her back against his chest. He spoke quietly, patiently. "You could never have done your route, Pepper. Your body experienced a shock yesterday. It needs time to recover."

Taking a deep breath, she let her head fall back to his shoulder. "It's betrayed me, this body has. I haven't taken a sick day since I've been on the job."

"Then you deserve one. And the postmaster understood completely. When I explained what had happened, he insisted you stay home. A man of my own thinking."

"Hmmmph. And he's not even in bed with us."

"Thank God," John murmured, shifting Pepper until she lay across his lap, in his arms. "You look pretty in the morning. Like a little elf with those freckles on your nose and your hair all over the place."

The freckles scrunched together when she made a face. "Elf?"

He cleared his throat. "More like a sexy siren, but I'm trying to stay cool. I've always been a morning person."

"I wondered," she said, then got his full meaning and blushed. His body was a wall of warmth supporting her. She was vibrantly aware of the subtle, but infinitely masculine, scent of his skin. "I, uh, John, maybe this isn't such a great idea. Maybe I ought to go home. I can rest there."

"You'll rest here. You owe me."

"I owe you?"

"For several hours of pure hell."

"I think you've got it backward. I ought to leave you in peace by way of thanks. Better still, I ought to finish hanging that damned wallpaper."

"You're not doing anything today," he said, laying her back on the pillow and bounding from bed, "but resting." She saw that he was wearing a slim pair of briefs and couldn't drag her eyes from the sight of him walking toward the bathroom. His body was magnificent. Her heart began to palpitate; she wished it were an aftershock from the sting but knew better.

Pulling the sheet to her chin, she listened to the sound of water running in the sink, then the shower. When John emerged from the bathroom, he wore nothing but a towel slung low on his hips. The palpitations began again.

"How're ya doin'?" he asked with a smile, coming to sit beside her. He handed her a pill, then a glass of water.

"Okay," she murmured, taking the pill, washing it down with the water. She saw that he'd shaved; his jaw was clean and smooth. Before she could reach out to touch him, though, he'd taken the glass from her and was off the bed again, headed for his dresser. He removed clean underwear and shorts. When the towel fell from his hips, Pepper closed her eyes, but the image of his firm buttocks remained, tantalizing her nearly as much as the quiet sounds of his dressing.

His feet padded softly across the wood floor moments before the mattress dipped again. "You can open your eyes now," he teased.

She did and pouted. "That was quite a stunt. Have you no sense of decency?"

"In my own bedroom . . . ? What would you like for breakfast?"

"You," she said on impulse. "Fried in butter, over easy."

"Done," he said with a grin, then was gone. When he returned, he was carefully balancing a large plate, napkins, utensils and juice. "Sorry I don't have a tray, but a man living alone doesn't have much cause for things like that."

Pepper pushed herself higher on the pillows. "No problem. When everything spills on the sheets, you'll have a permanent reminder of your stint as Florence Nightingale."

"She's feeling better," John murmured under his breath. He set down the plate, which bore four eggs and as many slices of toast, then handed her the juice and a fork, keeping one for himself.

"I thought you didn't cook."

"What I said was that I didn't cook when I could help it. Today, I can't help it. You need nourishment."

Evidently so did he, if the share of breakfast he himself ate was any indication. When the plate was clean, he set it on the nearby stand. "That was good, if I do say so myself."

"It was. Thank you," she said with quiet solemnity. "I don't believe I've ever had anyone wait on me before."

Leaning forward, he captured her lips in a long, lingeringly gentle kiss. "I don't believe I've ever waited on anyone before. I kinda like it."

She raised her hand then and explored the smoothness of his jaw. "You're a sweet man, John Smith."

"Is that all?"

"Sweet, and kind, and . . . and . . ."

"Virile?"

"That, too."

His second kiss was more thorough and spoke of that virility in countless ways. By the time it ended, Pepper was beginning to wonder just how weak she really was. When John kissed her, she felt strong and alive. When he kissed her, it was as though she hadn't a care in the world.

"I think . . . you'd better rest," he managed with some hoarseness when he finally pushed himself from the bed.

"What are you going to do?" she returned urgently.

"Hang wallpaper."

"Without me?" she called to his retreating back.

"You rest!" was all he said before he disappeared down the hall.

Pepper wasn't sure if she could rest. As spent as her body felt, her mind was working double time telling her she shouldn't let John pamper her, telling her she shouldn't feel as comfortable in his bed, telling her she should get up, get dressed, go back to her own bed where she belonged.

In the end, her body won. Head tucked into the pillow, she dozed off, awakening two hours later to the sound of a choice epithet coming from the bathroom down the hall. Slipping from bed, she followed the sound. John stood in the doorway of the bathroom they'd begun the day before. He was staring disgustedly at the walls.

"What's wrong?" she asked, coming up from behind and softly wrapping an arm around his waist.

"Look."

It took her but a minute to identify the problem. "Oh, no." She tried not to laugh. "Well, you did match it up perfectly."

"Yeah. The lines are all matched up. Too bad the pattern's upside down."

"You could always leave it that way. It'd be . . . interesting."

He looked down at her. "It's all your fault. If I hadn't been thinking of you lying all warm and docile in my bed. . . ." His tone gentled. "Did you sleep?"

"Mmm. Just woke up."

He arched backward and looked down. "The legs seem to be working. How do you feel?"

"Better."

"Still weak?"

"A little. Is that . . . normal?"

"The doctor said you'd be under the weather for a day or so. I think it's time for another pill."

"Those things knock me out."

"They've also done wonders for your hives. And besides, you need to sleep."

"Sure. To wear off the effect of the pills. It's a vicious circle."

Draping an arm around her shoulders, John propelled her back to bed. "Complain, complain, complain. You must be feeling better."

She didn't fight him, but took the pill he gave her and made herself comfortable while he went back to work. She dozed again, rousing to have the soup that he heated before she fell asleep once more.

It was midafternoon when she woke up, this time feeling well enough to crave a bath. As though John had anticipated her need, she found a set of fresh towels in the bathroom. She saw that the tub had been scrubbed clean. The only thing missing was a packet of her favorite jasmine bath salts. Smiling at how easily she could be spoiled, she ran a hot bath, then sank into the water and willed away the last of her stiffness.

The water had begun to turn tepid when at last she stepped out and toweled herself dry. Her shorts and T-shirt were nowhere in sight, so she slipped her panties back on, then John's shirt.

Back in bed, she was beginning to feel slightly hypocritical when John appeared at the door. He was wearing shorts and sneakers and a faded T-shirt that had been cropped well above his waist.

"Have a nice bath?"

"Mmm. Thank you."

"Don't thank me. Thank the plumber. He was the one who installed the new hot-water heater last week."

"Then my thanks go to him. It felt good."

"I'm glad." He came to sit beside her, lifting a hand to tuck damp tendrils of hair behind her ear. "You look rosy. Much more healthy."

"I feel it. John, maybe I ought to be getting back—"

"Shhh. Not yet."

"But I can't stay—"

"You can. For a little while longer." His silver gaze shimmered over her, leaving tingles wherever it touched. "I'm done for the day," he murmured, suddenly preoccupied with her lips. He ran a light finger over their soft curves, then, when they parted helplessly, touched the moist inner flesh.

What Pepper was feeling should have taken her very much by surprise, but it didn't. She was in John's bed, wearing little but his shirt, and there was nowhere else she'd rather be. That his nearness, his light touch, could send such waves of longing through her boggled her mind, but she couldn't fight him. Nor could she fight the sharp awareness that she hadn't yet seen the far reaches of his passion.

Her name was a mere whisper on his lips moments before they covered hers, and she was only aware of the rightness of it all, of the sense of well-being his body conveyed to hers. Threading his fingers into the dampness of her hair, he held her face firm as his kiss deepened. His lips opened wider; hers followed suit. Their tongues met and parried, each sliding the length of the other's with sensuous intent.

"So sweet," he murmured, pressing her down on the sheets, following her until, braced on his elbows, he loomed above. When his head lowered, she raised hers to meet it, using everything he'd taught her to heighten the sensations flowing through her body. His fingers went to the buttons of the shirt, releasing one, then another, until the fabric lay open. Propping himself up, he spread the shirt wide.

"What are you doing?" she whispered breathlessly.

"Looking at you. I don't think I'll ever see enough. You're so lovely."

She did feel lovely beneath his gaze and could no more have covered herself than she could, at that moment, have denied the fact that the sentiment was returned. Her hands found their way under his T-shirt and pushed it higher. In an instant he whipped the offending material over his head. Then, gathering her to him with the utmost care, he lifted her from the bed to press her breasts against his bare flesh.

A deep moan came from his throat. "I've never felt you this way. Oh, sweetheart, do you have any idea . . . ?"

"I do," she breathed. "I do." It was as heady a sensation for her, the feel of skin on skin, of curves on muscle. When he gently moved her so that her breasts rubbed against him, it was her turn to moan. The slight friction created an almost unbearable tension within her. She arched closer.

Once more John pressed her back to the bed, this time coming down full length on top of her. She felt his arousal and was all the more incited by it. The knowledge that she held the power to stimulate him so fully was heady indeed.

Threading his fingers through hers, he anchored them by her shoulders. He kissed her hungrily, rocking his long body against hers in a way that stole her breath. Then, raising his hips just a fraction, he took her hand and urged it lower.

Suddenly frightened, she resisted.

"Touch me," he whispered. "Just once. Don't be afraid. I won't hurt you." His hand was persistent and, bidden by curiosity and an utterly feminine need, she allowed him to press her fingers to the cloth that shielded his hardness. "There," he moaned. "There. My God, Pepper, I've needed you to touch me. Here, I'll show you...."

He slid her hand gently up and down, showing her how to please him, removing his own only when her fingers spread more boldly and took the initiative. His lips caught hers, tongue thrusting deeply as his hips mimed the action against her hand.

"You drive me crazy," he whispered roughly, sliding lower until his face was buried between her breasts. He moved his head from one side to the other, and Pepper thought she'd go mad for wanting him to kiss her breasts. When she could take the torment no longer, she cupped his head in her hands and guided it. His lips opened over her nipple. He sucked strongly then, and she cried out in response. When he moved to the other breast, she began to writhe against him.

"Feel good?" he asked, his breath hot on her flesh.

"Oh, yes. I want...."

His lips trailed flame to her neck. "What? Tell me, sweetheart. Tell me what you want."

She wanted the pot of gold at the end of the rainbow. She wanted the answer to why she was made a woman. She wanted the end to this furnace of heat between her legs. But she could barely speak, her breath seemed in such short supply. "I want...."

He slipped his hand into her panties and slid the silken fabric down her legs. Then, releasing the snap and zipper of his shorts on the return trip, he was over her once again. His lips found hers, his fingers found her lower warmth. Each opened, each caressed.

Suddenly she was a woman aching for total possession. She ran her fingers over his damp skin, probing lower to the point where his shorts began. He arched up only enough to reach down and release himself, then took her hand and closed it over his erection.

Stunned by his heat, she nearly demurred. But his urgent murmurings gave her courage to caress him. With a deep growl, he withdrew from her only to kick off his sneakers and pants, then he was back, finding his place between her legs, thrusting upward.

She arched at the sharp sting of pain and panted softly.

"Pepper...my God!" he gasped, trying to control himself, trying to understand what he'd felt. "I didn't...I can't...stop...."

"Don't," she cried. "Please...go on."

"But I've hurt you...."

"No. It's all right." Already the pain had eased, yielding to a warm expectancy. "Oh...John...."

Arms trembling as he held his chest from hers, he kissed the corners of her mouth. "Tip your hips up...it'll feel better...that's it...."

With infinite care, he began to move inside her, withdrawing slowly, returning ever more deeply until he could feel from the motion of her hips that she was experiencing pleasure. He grew bolder then, moving more rapidly, tempering his thrusts to the cadence of her breathing. He tried to remember that she was torn inside, but his own need was so great that he strained unsuccessfully.

"I can't . . . hold back."

Bringing her head from the pillow, she stilled his lips with her own. When he stiffened, then cried out, she knew a sense of instinctive satisfaction that a woman can know only when her man has reached the pinnacle of passion. The fact that a tiny part of her still craved the same pinnacle was secondary to the fact of the pleasure that she, untutored and raw, had been able to give. For the time being, the rhythmic pulsation of John's climax within her was pleasure enough.

At long last, he collapsed over her. His skin was wet, his breathing ragged. She welcomed the intimacy that his weight brought and was disappointed when he slid carefully to her side.

"Pepper," he breathed. Her name echoed in the room for long moments. "You should have told me."

Embarrassed, she tried to bury her face against his chest, but he wouldn't have it. Grasping her chin between his thumb and forefinger, he tipped it up. His eyes burned into hers.

"I would have been more gentle. I had no idea you were a virgin."

She winced at the word. "I told you that I had never . . . that night at the drive-in."

"I didn't realize you were talking about this . . . this whole thing. I thought you just meant—"

"John, please, I feel like an idiot."

"Idiot?" he murmured, brushing his lips against her brow before settling her in the crook of his shoulder. "Not by a long shot. You were—you are—beautiful. And you have no idea how much it means to me that you were a . . . that you've never been with another man. I just assumed—I mean, you are twenty-seven." When she said nothing, he prodded, "Why, Pepper? Why have there been no men before me?"

She shrugged. "I never felt . . . the urge."

"Never? But you're so filled with passion."

"I guess I've never met anyone who brought it out."

He let out a loud breath. "Well, you have now, and before this night's over, you're going to feel what I just felt. Over and over again." His voice lowered to a near whisper. "I love you, Pepper. You know that, don't you?"

Pepper stiffened.

"DON'T SAY THAT," she cried, pushing herself to a sitting position with the urgency of pure emotion. When John's eyes went wide, she lowered her voice. "Don't say that."

"Why not? I mean it."

"No." Closing her eyes, she shook her head. "You don't mean it. Please."

A tiny voice inside told him he should have seen it coming. The signs were all there in her past, topped off by the fact that, until this day, she'd never let any man touch her deepest heart. What had she said...? That she'd never had the urge before. There was a remote possibility that she did, indeed, see the act as something totally physical. More probably, he realized, she would refuse to recognize the deeper feelings that had permitted his penetration of her body, if not her soul.

"Would it be so awful?" he ventured softly.

His voice washed over her like a warm, soothing wave and she had to steel herself against its lure. Turning her back, she huddled into herself. "I don't want to talk about it."

"You've got to, because it exists. Would it be so awful...my loving you?"

"Love ruins things. It hurts. It doesn't last."

"You're speaking of your parents, and that's not necessarily—"

"I'm speaking of so many of the people I've met over the years, people who thought they were in love and then discovered differently."

"I'm not asking for commitment, Pepper. I simply wanted you to know how I felt. I've known for a long time. I should have said it before."

"You should have."

"And you never would have let today happen?"

"I never would have let a lot of todays happen. I can't love you back. Don't you see?"

"Can't? Or won't?"

"Does it matter?"

"To me it does. Can't is something irrevocable. Won't means I've still got a chance."

"You haven't got a chance."

He was sitting up behind her, his voice low and firm. "I don't believe that."

"It's a fact."

"Not quite." When he put his hand on her shoulder, she pulled away. But he simply lunged forward and had her flat on her back with her hands pinned to the sheets before she could flee. "I'm not letting you go," he stated calmly. "You may have scared all the other guys away with that speech—"

"I've never *used* it on another guy."

"Which goes a long way in making my point. You've never let another man touch you, but you let me. Don't you think that says something about your emotional involvement?"

She squeezed her eyes shut, trying desperately to block out his words. She didn't want to hear them, didn't want to think about them.

"Hell, Pepper, I'd say you're up to your pretty little ears this time. You can go home to your lonely bed, but you won't be able to forget what happened here."

"I'll find diversions."

"With another man? Who are you trying to kid? I always sensed there was something innocent about you. And I refuse to believe it's because guys haven't tried to break through. I made it. Me. There's a reason. . . . Oh, God, don't do that. . . ." A single tear had escaped her clenched lids, then another. "Don't cry, sweetheart. I don't want to make you unhappy."

Sniffing, she turned her head sideways on the pillow. "It was so beautiful, seeing you every day. . . . And what happened today. . . . I wanted it. But I can't. . . . I don't want . . . to think. . . ."

"Okay," he whispered quickly. "Okay." He drew her up, cradling her in his arms, pressing her wet cheek to his chest. "We won't think. We'll just keep on doing what we've been doing. I can wait. I told you. I'm a patient man."

Pepper wasn't sure what was wrong with her but she couldn't seem to stop crying. Soft sobs persisted, sliding from her throat to be muffled by the light furring of hair on John's chest.

"When was the last time you cried?" he asked quietly.

"I . . . don't know."

"See. That should show you—" When she tried to pull away, he caught himself. "Shhh. I won't say any more. Just stay here. Just relax." His hand stroked her back, gliding from her shoulder down her spine to spread over her hips. "Shhh." He rocked her gently. Slowly she quieted and he kissed the warm crown of her head.

"John . . ." she began, wanting to tell him something but not sure what.

"Shhh. It's okay. Just stay here and remember how nice it was a little while ago. Did you like it . . . when I filled you?" She nodded against his head. "And that's just the beginning. The first time's always hardest for a woman. If you felt pleasure then, just think of what you'll feel when I make love to you again. You have no idea how good it was for me."

"Was it?" she asked in a meek voice. More than once it had occurred to her that, inexperienced as she was, she'd be lacking in some way. "Did I do it . . . right?"

"Oh, yes," he breathed. "You did it right because you're a very passionate woman. Instinct guided you, told you that what you were feeling was right. And you wanted to please me." He wanted to say that she was acting out her love, but didn't dare. "Innocence and desire make a fantastic combination."

"Have you had many . . . virgins before?"

"Just one."

"Was she good?"

"I don't really know. I was a virgin, too, then. We were seventeen. We fumbled a lot."

Pepper laughed. It wasn't the self-confident, oft-mischievous laugh he was used to hearing, but it was a laugh nonetheless. She slid a hand down to rub the back of her knee. "I can't imagine you ever fumbling."

"How did you think I learned?"

"I can picture some femme fatale being totally taken with your youthful virility." She tipped her head back and grinned more naturally. "An older woman—maybe twenty-nine or thirty—craving your puberty-fresh body, taking you under her wing, tutoring you on her satin sofa in the sultry heat of an August afternoon."

"You've got quite an imagination," John said, then laughed aloud. "It wasn't that way, believe me."

"No older women?"

"Nope."

"No satin sofas?"

"Nope."

"No sultry August afternoons?"

John's smile faded and his gaze grew lambent. "Only this one," he murmured throatily, then lowered his head and kissed the warm lips awaiting his.

If Pepper had thought to flee his arms, she no longer did. One touch of his mouth on hers and she was mesmerized. He was a skillful lover, intuitively sensing what she needed. His lips slid, then clung, then caressed with such fierce tenderness that she was enraptured anew. He was a charmer, and charm her he did until her own mouth was pliant, then active, ardently returning his kiss.

Pepper was aware of so many more things this time. She relished the rich, vital thickness of his hair as she combed her finger through and held him to her breast. She thrilled to the bunching of the muscles of his back when he raised himself to probe lower. She reveled in the fluid heat that filled her veins and made her body weep for want of his. And when her fingertips skidded down his steeply arched back as he held himself poised at the brink of entrance, she knew that, whatever the future might bring, she would have this magnificence to remember.

He spoke in a hoarse, broken whisper. "There...you're ready for me, sweetheart...it won't hurt this time."

It didn't. He moved with infinite care, introducing himself to her tender sheath by inches, all the while alternating between soft, sweet verbal murmurings and the gentlest, most riveting of kisses. When he was deep, deep inside, he paused to savor the expression on Pepper's face. He saw amazement there, and pleasure, and yes, love, though she would deny it. When he smiled, she smiled back. When he swooped down to steal her lips, she met him halfway. And then there was no denying the intense joy they both felt, for it was expressed in helpless cries and sighs and writhings.

For Pepper, the upset of moments before was gone, replaced by a sense of wholeness, of unity, of rapture so great that she soared high above any plane she'd ever reached before. As John's thrusts quickened, so did the beat of her pulse. She matched his movements, surging with the growing coil of delicious tension deep within, straining higher, ever higher, until, in one blinding moment, accompanied by his triumphant cry, her insides exploded and she clung to him, trembling as he did, gasping likewise.

It seemed an eternity before the aftershocks slowed and they fell back to the bed. Their bodies were slick, spent, intertwined with each other though clearly devoid of strength.

John said nothing, but a slow smile of satisfaction worked its way to his lips when at last he turned his damp head toward hers. Her eyes were wide open and filled with awe.

"That was," she whispered, still trying to catch her breath, "that was unbelievable!"

His grin widened. He took the weight of his body on an elbow, though his long legs remained locked with Pepper's. "When it's good, it's good. Our bodies respond perfectly to each other. I knew it would be that way—"

"When? When did you know?"

"The second day, when you came with the mail and had a drink with me. I touched your ankle and knew."

"My ankle? There's nothing sensual about my ankle."

"Wanna bet? You felt it, too. Don't deny it. And then, the day I was scraping paint from the house and you brushed some of the dust from my chest?"

She gave a lopsided grin. "I thought I'd been burned."

"You had, but by fire of a different sort than the usual. Of course—" he licked the corner of his mouth "—then there are the backs of your knees."

"What about the backs of my knees?"

"They're very sensitive."

"Now, wait a minute. You've never *touched* the backs of my knees."

"No, but you have. You rub one or the other whenever we're together. At first I thought it was nervousness. But it's not. I think it's the precursor of another itch. . . . I'd show you, if I weren't so damned dead."

She smiled, though her brows knit. The overall effect was one of skeptical delight. "Do you really think that the backs of my knees are that sensitive?"

"I'd put money on it."

"Will you . . . test it some time?"

Her shy question put John in seventh heaven. It implied that he and Pepper had a future. And as long as they had that, there was hope. "It'd be my pleasure," he stated unequivocably. "My pleasure."

OVER JOHN'S OBJECTION, Pepper returned to work the following morning. "I'm sorry," she teased, holding her palms up straight, "but I simply have to go. I don't think my boss would buy raw lust as an adequate reason to stay in bed." John was, indeed, still in bed. Pepper had awoken particularly early, knowing she'd have to get home and dress.

"You could tell him you're still sick."

She was looking around. "Where are my shorts?"

"I washed them. They're downstairs on top of the dryer. Tell him *I'm* sick. I will be, if you leave."

"That little boy act won't work, John Smith," she called from the hall as she headed downstairs. When she returned, he was no more acclimated to her leaving.

"Come on, Pep. You can't be feeling up to snuff. Hell, it was less than forty-eight hours ago that you nearly died from a bee sting!"

She dug through the bed clothes for her panties but realized that they hadn't been washed with the rest. "I didn't nearly die. And you're a fine one to be worrying in hindsight. If you'll recall, it was less than twenty-four hours ago that—" she bent down to enunciate by his ear "—you took my virginity." She dodged away just in time to escape his lunging arm.

"But that's another reason why you should stay here. You've got to be sore." The gingerly way she was stepping into her shorts gave evidence to his claim. But suddenly he wasn't thinking of her soreness. His eyes widened. "God, Pepper, you're not wearing underpants!"

She carefully zipped up her shorts. "I'll get fresh ones at home when I change."

With a moan, John closed his eyes and drew his knees up. "I can't believe this. Yesterday afternoon, all last night . . . and I think of you like that and. . . ."

Pepper's laugh was muffled beneath her T-shirt. "You can work it off." Though she didn't dare admit it for fear he'd make a successful lunge at her and quash her good intentions, seeing John in bed that way, covered in the most token of manners by the thinnest of sheets, was making her throb inside. Or was that the soreness he spoke of? She could feel it at the insides of her thighs and was counting on a long, hot jasmine soak to ease her stiffness.

"Will I see you tonight?" he asked then, all playfulness gone.

Pepper looked at him for a minute. The tiny voice inside her said she shouldn't. But the tiny voice couldn't see the longing on his face. The tiny voice couldn't see the taunting pattern of hair tapering from his chest to his belly. The tiny voice couldn't possibly know the pleasure his lovemaking had brought.

"If you'd like," she answered softly.

"I'd like. Dinner?"

"I'll cook. About seven."

"Six."

"Six-thirty." Turning, she headed for the stairs. "And not a minute earlier, or you'll find yourself with a TV dinner."

THE NEXT WEEK was a strange one for Pepper. When she was with John—every night plus all day Sunday and Thursday—she was ecstatic. He never mentioned love again, which pleased her. And their relationship was as warm, as fun, as companionable as it had ever been— with the addition of a fiery passion that seemed to know no end. Each time they made love it was better than the last. She learned what John liked, what turned him on most. And she learned that the backs of her knees were, indeed, exquisitely erotic spots.

When she was alone, well, that was another matter. She found herself brooding, pondering things she'd pushed from her mind for years. She would wander around her apartment deep in thought, feeling restless and frustrated and disturbed. She'd conclude that she had to stop seeing John, but it never took more than the sound of his voice or the sight of his face to change her mind. Indeed, all she had to do was to walk down Casey Lane making deliveries to find that her pulse sped a little more with each stop. She was like one of Pavlov's dogs, she mused; her body had been conditioned to throb in the mere anticipation of seeing John.

True to his word, John got tickets for Tanglewood. They drove up the following weekend, leaving the instant she'd finished rushing through her route on Saturday, arriving in time to catch the evening's concert, then the one scheduled for Sunday afternoon. They spent the night at a nearby inn, which Pepper declared was every bit as inspiring as Beethoven. Taking that as the supreme compliment, John was delighted.

Things were going very much as he'd hoped. He knew Pepper loved him, could see it in her eyes whenever they were together. He also imagined the soul-searching she was doing when she was away from him and felt the slightest bit of trepidation on that score. But she responded to everything he did, and she was dynamite in bed. Very often, she was the one to initiate their love-making. She seemed to need him as badly as he needed her. It was a step toward cementing their future. He could only hope that he could get under her skin and into her soul so fully that she'd be unable to conceive of life without him.

Conceive. He thought about that, too. In all the times he and Pepper had made love, he hadn't used any form of birth control. She'd been a virgin that first time and had very obviously been unprepared. To his knowledge, she'd done nothing to alter that fact. And he wasn't sorry. Though he knew that marriage spurred by pregnancy was risky business, he also knew that the love they shared would see the marriage to fruition. The thought of Pepper's bearing their child was a heady one indeed.

"My family's coming this weekend," he told her on the Tuesday evening after they'd returned from Tanglewood. "I'd like you to meet them."

They'd been sprawled, sipping soda, on a single lounge chair on John's newly awninged and screened porch. He felt her immediate glimmer of tension.

She hesitated. "I don't know, John. They'll be seeing the place for the first time. And you haven't visited them in a while. Maybe you'd rather be alone."

"I can see them just as well if you're here with me."

"But it'll be so busy. The last thing you need is another face around here."

"The first thing I need is yours. Then I can relax and enjoy theirs."

"Will the beds be in?" She knew that he'd ordered furniture several weeks before. "How many of them will there be—four adults, three kids?"

"Uh-huh." He was pleased that she remembered the exact count. "The beds are being delivered Thursday. Two pairs of twins for each of the larger bedrooms. The kids will camp out in sleeping bags on the floor of one of the other rooms."

"They won't mind? After all, they've been camping out all summer."

"A—you've never seen the camps they go to. And B— are you kidding? They'll have a ball exploring the house, choosing which little nook they want to sleep in. Knowing my nephews, they'll decide to bunk in the luggage compartment down the hall, or in the cedar closet in the attic. This house was made for kids." After the most pregnant of pauses, he got back to the point. "Will you come?"

Looking up at him then, she saw the same intense need that got to her every time. "I...I don't think I should stay here. I'd feel . . . awkward."

He grinned. "Sharing my bed? I'm a big boy. My parents would understand. In fact, they'd be thrilled. There are times when they worry that I'm alone."

"I couldn't. It wouldn't be right."

"Okay." His grin persisted. She was darling when her sense of morality exerted itself, which hadn't been that often, thank heavens. "Then just come during the days." He lowered his voice. "We can catch it on the sly, like when I drive you home at night."

"John Smith, you are incorrigible," she scolded, but she was smiling, too.

"Then you will?"

"I will. But I'm warning you—your parents may begin to *truly* worry about you when they discover that you're hung up on the mailman."

John hugged her tightly, realizing that there was more than a little insecurity in Pepper MacNeil. "I think I can work my way around that one," he crooned. "Very easily."

JOHN'S FAMILY was every bit as lovely as Pepper had feared, though she was in for several surprises when John picked her up and drove her back to his house late Saturday afternoon. The first was his mother. Pepper had correctly imagined her to be the kind of warm, loving person who'd raised John to be similarly inclined. What Pepper hadn't imagined was that the woman with the pixieish figure happened to be confined to a wheelchair.

"He didn't tell you," Kathleen Smith observed soon after she and Pepper were introduced. They were sitting on the porch watching a spontaneous game of baseball being played by the boys, their father, grandfather and John in the backyard. Pepper would have chosen to stay with the gentle-mannered woman even if it hadn't been for the fear—the first of her allergy shots notwithstanding—she'd developed of bees.

When Pepper turned to her in surprise, Mrs. Smith smiled. "I could see it in your eyes, just for a minute there at the start. He takes it for granted, my John does. We all do. It's been so long."

"What happened?" Pepper asked softly.

"I was hit by a car in a supermarket parking lot. Had my arms loaded with bundles and wasn't watching where I was going. I wasn't hit all that hard, just the wrong way. Monica was eight at the time, John six."

Pepper could begin to imagine the pain, though she'd never dreamed John's childhood had been marred in any way. "It must have been very hard—on all of you."

"It was, at first. But we adjusted. We had no choice. But tell me about you, Pepper. John says you're the mailman around here. Have you been here long?"

Feeling nearly as comfortable talking with his mother as she did with John, Pepper told her about work. When Mrs. Smith seemed genuinely intrigued and prodded further, Pepper found herself opening all the more. She'd covered the toll booth, the pub, and the gas station when the small woman in the wheelchair chuckled gaily.

"I bet you've never been a pinsetter in a bowling alley."

Pepper's brows rose. "Pinsetter?"

"It was in the days before automatics were put in, the days before I married Stuart. I had a wonderful time of it, climbing up and down, making friends with the fellows who came regularly to bowl. They were very protective. When I started seeing Stuart, they actually checked him out."

Pepper laughed. "That's amazing. Pinsetting! I'd never have thought of that one."

"You would have if you'd been born forty years earlier."

"Why did you do it?" Pepper asked curiously. She had a deep need to know.

"It was fun. It was steady. I met wonderful people. Isn't that why many of us work?"

"Then my own wild streak doesn't sound so bizarre to you?"

"Of course not. You have your reasons for doing what you do. And it shows a sense of adventure. I'm sure it's one of the things John loves about you. Ah—" she caught her breath, as Pepper did, but for a different reason "—here comes Monica." A slender woman wearing a billowing yellow sundress appeared at the door, bonnet in hand. "You look—" her mother selected her words with care "—sunny, as usual. I was wondering when you'd finally finish dressing. Pepper, dear, this is John's sister, Monica. Monica, Pepper MacNeil."

Slightly awed by the dazzling image before her, Pepper stood and smiled, but Monica would have no part of that. Wearing a grin that was every bit as bright as her outfit, she gave Pepper a warm hug. That was when Pepper received her second surprise of the day.

"I don't believe it," she murmured, sniffing the air experimentally as she held herself back from Monica. Her smile turned into a sheepish grin. "You're wearing lavender."

"I always do," Monica asserted with an impish shrug that somehow seemed to fit her, though she had to be approaching forty. "It's my trademark, in a way. I put it on everything. Too heavily sometimes, mother thinks, but I love it."

"You'll never believe what I thought," Pepper began. She and Monica continued to stand with their hands on each other's elbows. It seemed a perfectly natural, comfortable pose. "The first day I delivered mail to John, there was a lavender letter in the bunch. It had a flowery script—"

"And red ink?" Mrs. Smith injected dryly.

Pepper grinned. "Uh-huh. I assumed that John had a passionate lover back in New York."

Monica chuckled and glanced toward the yard. "I like to think of myself as a passionate lover, but, thank you, not John's." Abruptly, she released Pepper to run to the screen. "He was safe, daddy! I saw that play. Michael was safe at home!"

"Monica, your father's the umpire," Greg, her husband, informed her with mock sternness. "You can't argue with the umpire."

"Well, I can! That was a bad call! John, you saw it. Wasn't he safe?"

"I agree with Greg," John drawled. "The umpire has the final word."

Monica had put her bonnet on and was tying it under her chin. "That's because you're on the opposite team and you're losing!" She reached for the screen door. "Pepper, we'll talk a little later. These men don't know how to play baseball. Daddy," she called, running out in the yard, "you go out in the field. *I'll* be the umpire!"

It was just a sampling of what Pepper was to see that evening and all day Sunday. John's father, like John, was quiet and soft spoken, intelligent and easy to talk to. Monica and her mother added spice to the family. Monica's husband, obviously adoring his wife, enjoyed himself through it all. And the boys—well, the boys were as spirited as three preteens should be.

For Pepper, it was both a wonderful weekend and a disaster. With each passing hour she felt more torn apart until, when John drove her home on Sunday night, she was hard pressed to contain her heartache.

"Well," he said, killing the Scout's engine and turning to her, "what do you think?"

"I think they're wonderful," she said in such a soft voice that he eyed her askance.

"You don't sound sure. Monica didn't say anything dumb, did she? Her tongue sometimes gets away from her—"

"Oh, no. Monica was terrific. I felt very close to her." It was true. The two had spent much time talking. Pepper could have easily pictured her as the sister she'd never had but always wanted.

"Then what is it, sweetheart?"

His voice took on an aching lilt. He could read her so well. It wasn't fair. She scrounged around within herself for vestiges of strength.

"Nothing." She forced a smile, but it barely touched her lips before fading. "I guess I'm just tired, that's all."

Heart skipping a beat, John put both hands on her shoulders and turned her to him. "Are you feeling all right?"

"Yes. Yes. Just tired."

His hopes rose. Fatigue was the first sign. "Are you . . . do you think. . . . I mean, we haven't used anything . . . do you think you might be pregnant?"

It was the final straw. One part of her—an irrational part, but a persistent one nonetheless—had hoped upon hope that it might be true, but it wasn't. On top of everything else, having to admit this to John now was devastating. She felt more empty, more alone at that moment than she'd ever remembered feeling.

"No," she said, swallowing hard, "I'm not pregnant." To her dismay, her eyes began to fill with tears. "I've got to go," she whispered, tucking her head low and opening the door of the Scout.

John reached her when she was halfway to her front door. Taking her arm, he forced her to stop. "Pepper, talk to me. Something's bothering you and I have to know what it is."

"You don't *have* to know." She raised moist eyes. "You're not my keeper."

"But I care, sweetheart. More than you can believe. I love you." When she flinched and tore out of his grasp, he was instantly after her. She'd just reached the door when he stopped in front to bar her entrance. "I know you don't like to hear that, but it's true. And to love means to worry. If something happened this weekend, if something about my family bothered you, I want to know."

Pepper hated herself for crying, but she couldn't help it. She felt as though her heart was being squeezed and wrung, pulled in two directions at once. The pain was excruciating.

"Nothing happened," she cried, tears streaming down her face. "I loved your family. They did everything right.

It's just me. Please, John. I want to go in. I need to be alone."

Very slowly he stood aside to let her pass, but he followed her in. She was confused and upset, but his state was quickly matching hers. "I don't like this, Pepper. I've never seen you this way. Something's wrong, dammit! Tell me!"

Grasping the post at the bottom of the loft stairs, she turned. Her cheeks were wet; her eyes, anguish filled. Never before in her life had she begged, but she did it now in a voice as heartrending as any John had ever heard. "Leave, John. Please. If you love me, respect the need I have to be alone just now."

"I don't understand this," he moaned, rubbing his hand along the back of his neck. "I don't understand it at all."

What meager composure Pepper had was fading by the minute. She pressed her fingers to her upper lip. "Please?" she whispered. "Your parents will be waiting."

"Then they'll wait! This is too important—"

"*John!*" she screamed, shaking all over. "*Go!*"

He raked his fingers through his hair. It was clear to him that Pepper did need to be alone. Loving her, he had to respect that need. "All right. But I'll call you later."

"No! Not tonight. I need...I need...." When her legs would hold her no longer, she collapsed on the bottommost stair. "Go," she whispered from behind the hands that covered her face.

Leaving Pepper in the state she was in was the hardest thing that John had ever had to do in his life, but he did it. Against his better judgment, against every fiber in him that urged him to take her in his arms and shake the truth out of her, he turned around and left. Knowing that he couldn't face his family in the state he himself was in, he drove around for several hours. His family would assume he was with Pepper; there was no need to spoil the illusion.

His parents had taken to her instantly, as had his sister and her family. "She adores you, old man," his brother-in-law had said that afternoon. "I think you've got one to stick to for life. Good show."

John had believed him. He still believed him. Making Pepper believe it was going to be the hard part.

When he finally arrived home, the house was mercifully quiet. The first thing he did was try to call Pepper. Her line was busy. He waited for five minutes and tried again, with similar results. Ten, fifteen, twenty minutes later it was still busy. When he tried for what had to have been the tenth time, a full hour after he'd returned, and found no change, he accepted the fact that she'd taken the receiver off the hook.

It was all he could do to keep calm, to tell himself that she was all right, that she just needed to be alone. Lying in bed, wide awake and distraught, he went over everything that had happened that weekend, trying to understand what it was that had snapped in Pepper's mind. He couldn't understand it; things had been so good. It was as though he'd been living in a dream for the past two weeks, a dream that was suddenly shattered.

Dawn had fully broken over the eastern sky when he came to the only possible conclusion. Pepper was terrified—terrified of love, terrified of being hurt. She'd as much as said it that evening after they'd first made love, when he'd declared his feelings. As long as he hadn't pressed her, she'd been fine. Unfortunately, his family had been the embodiment of everything she might have, and lose, if her theory was correct.

But it wasn't! She was wrong, so very wrong. He loved her; he'd *always* be there for her. He knew his family would feel the same.

Sprawling over the bed that suddenly seemed far too large and empty, he grabbed the phone and dialed her number. It wasn't busy this time. Nor was it being answered. After fifteen rings he hung up, assuming she was in the bath.

For the first time in long hours of agony, he smiled. She loved to bathe. Even now closing his eyes, he could smell her. Jasmine sorcery, that's what it was. He'd been bewitched.

Snapping open his eyes, he tried her number again. But she'd still be in the tub. Long baths were her passion . . . well, among other things. Again he smiled and, crossing his hands behind his head, stretched out on the bed. He was convinced that, with the night and a leisurely soak behind her, she'd be more calm. He would talk with her then. He would confront her with his suspicions. Perhaps he'd been too indulgent, too gentle. This time, he'd take the bull by the horns.

He actually dozed off, awakening to the sound of the boys squabbling far down the hall. It was nearly seven-thirty. He dialed Pepper's number again. The phone rang and rang and rang. He must have missed her; she often went to work early when she wanted to finish early. That was it; she was rushing so that she might be free to be with him later. Things were going to be all right. He knew it!

His family left shortly after nine, loading up the car and starting the long journey home. There were warm hugs all around, and just as many goodbyes left for Pepper. When the house was quiet once more, John busied himself cleaning up, then stationed himself on the front steps, reading the newspaper, waiting for Pepper to come with the mail.

She didn't come. Already uneasy when ten, then ten-thirty had come and gone with no sign of her, John stiffened when he saw Will round the corner and start up the drive. He was quickly on his feet, running forward.

"Where's Pepper?" he asked, too frightened to hear how imperious his tone was.

Though too much of a Maine man to be ruffled, Will eyed him strangely. "I dunno. I got a call to come in early this morning. Postmaster didn't explain."

"Is she sick?" John demanded, then answered himself. "You don't know. Okay." He took his mail with a low-murmured "Thanks" and headed back to the house on the run. Instinct told him to hurry; he listened and obeyed.

He headed for Pepper's place first. When no one answered his repeated knocks, he drove straight to the post office. An odd premonition filled him with dread. His muscles tensed; his palms grew damp. It was the postmaster who verified his fears.

"She's gone," he said with a shrug. "Called me at the crack of dawn to say that she had to leave the area."

"Gone." A part of John curled up inside and died. "Are you sure?" But he knew it was true without asking; his voice was weighted down in defeat.

"Sure as I can be, seein' as Pepper's never lied to me yet. She was a good girl, that one. Not here too long, but she was one of the brightest faces we had 'round here for years."

"Gone." John struggled to gather his wits. His throat grew tight. He cleared it and blinked. "Did she say where she was going? Did she give any forwarding address?"

"Nope. Don't think she had one. She sounded kind of . . . upset, you know what I mean?"

"I know what you mean. But . . . what about her pay? Surely there's money coming to her. You'll have to send it somewhere."

"We didn't talk 'bout that. She was in a kind of rush. I 'sume she'll be back in touch when she knows where she's goin'."

John tried to curb his runaway imagination. "Listen, could you do me a favor?" Grabbing a small pad of paper from the table nearby, he began to write. "This is my name, address and phone number. I've specifically marked it Re: Pepper MacNeil. If you hear anything, even the smallest thing, will you let me know?" He held out the paper. "It's urgent."

The postmaster ignored the piece of paper to squint at John. "You're the fella bought the Fletcher place, aren't you?"

"That's right. And it's *absolutely urgent* that you let me know if you hear from Pepper."

"Why?"

John would have laughed at the man's bluntness if he hadn't been so torn up inside. "Because I love her," he murmured, slapping the paper down in front of the man. Then, trusting his composure no further, he fled to the Scout.

Hands white knuckled on the steering wheel, he took a series of deep breaths. Only when his vision cleared did he start off. Even then his mind was in such turmoil that he nearly missed his turn. When he got home, he walked into the house and stood in the large front hall. His head fell back; he closed his eyes against the pain that surged through every inch of his being.

Taking a deep, shuddering breath, he straightened and tried to think of where she might go. She had no roots. She could be headed anywhere, could do anything. How could he find her?

A sense of weariness washed over him. Almost absently, he picked up the mail he'd dropped so carelessly on the small table by the door. Bills, a notice that his membership was due to the counselor's association. He caught his breath. A small white envelope bearing his name and nothing else. . . .

Heart pounding in his chest, he tore at the sealed flap. His hands shook as he unfolded the letter. Then he died another little death.

"Dear John. . . ."

8

DEAR JOHN, I may be a coward of the first order for not being able to face you, but I couldn't leave without somehow saying goodbye. It's time for me to move on. You were right; I'm in over my head here. I only hope that in time you'll forgive me for what I've done.

You deserve better, far better than anything I could give you. You're a wonderful man with a heart of gold, and you need a woman, a wife who can give you both the love you want and a house full of kids. I can't.

I want you to know that I'll never forget any one of the moments we spent together. They will be with me always, as will the hope that you find what you're looking for some day soon.

It was signed, simply, "Pepper," but there was a scraggly postscript at the bottom. "Why not give either Pamela Hoffman or Jenna Lloyd a call—they're both wonderful. It would do my heart good to know that you were in caring hands."

John's arm fell limply to his side, and when he looked up grief was etched on his features. He managed to walk to the staircase, then collapse onto one of the lower steps, where he sat, knees spread, Pepper's letter dangling loosely between them. His life seemed suddenly dark, dreary. He couldn't imagine a future without Pepper.

Lifting the letter to his nose, he breathed in the scent that he'd always associate with her. Jasmine. Sweet, haunting, stirring his insides as it had from the start.

His body began to shake and he took long, harsh gulps of air. It was so stupid, all so stupid! Two lives...wasted! She had no right, dammit, no right at all to do this to either him or herself!

Anger rose in him like a thundercloud, threatening explosion, in dire need of release. Bounding from the stair, he stuffed the letter in his pocket on his way out the door. He was going to find her if it was the last thing he ever did!

It was easier said than done.

He went first to her landlord, knocking on the door of the house adjacent to her garage apartment. A pleasant looking woman, middle-aged and neat, opened the door, recognizing him immediately. Though they'd never been formally introduced, she knew him as the man who'd spent so much time with Pepper. Local gossip had told her more. He didn't have to say much by way of explaining his presence; the anguish on his face said it all.

"Did she speak with you today?" he asked, trying to keep calm.

The woman nodded. "She stopped by early this morning on her way out. She looked terrible. Very tired. And she'd been crying."

Cold fingers circled John's heart and squeezed. "What did she say?"

"She said she had to leave, but that she was paying the rent through September. She said she'd make some arrangement to get her things by then."

"She left everything?"

"I don't know, really. It's not my, uh—since she's paid the rent, I didn't feel it my place to explore."

"Could I? I mean, I won't disturb anything. But I've got to find her, and there may be a clue."

There wasn't. Her apartment was exactly as it had always been. She appeared to have taken nothing but her clothes. Even her stereo was there. She'd obviously been in a rush.

John did contact both Pam Hoffman and Jenna Lloyd, but not for the purpose Pepper had intended. Neither woman knew of her disappearance; both were stunned. He spent hours talking with each, going over and over any detail they could offer about Pepper's past, in the hope that some small thing might suggest where she'd gone. Nothing did.

He spent the evening at home, praying that Pepper might have second thoughts and call. When she didn't, he debated going to the police to place a missing persons report. But he couldn't do that. She was an adult, and as such was free to go where she liked. The police wouldn't be terribly sympathetic to his cause, and he was sure that

Pepper, law-abiding citizen that she was, would do nothing to attract the attention of the authorities in other states.

Early the next morning, he visited the postmaster again, only to find that there had been no word from Pepper. It took some convincing on John's part before the postmaster showed him her employment application, on which were listed the addresses and phone numbers of the places she'd worked previously. He spent the day making calls, but learned nothing other than that she'd been well liked wherever she'd been. Not one person had seen her, not one even knew she'd been working in Maine. Not one had the vaguest idea where she might be. At each place he left his name and number on the chance that someone might hear something, but he knew enough not to raise his hopes. Pepper had established a clear pattern of cutting ties, of leaving without a trace. He feared she was too adept at it to slip up now.

On his third morning alone, he drove into Portland to meet with a private investigator. Whereas John was an amateur at hunting people down, this man was an expert. John prayed he'd come up with a new angle.

He didn't. He listened patiently to everything John told him, asking questions here and there, but his conclusion was far from optimistic.

"I could take your money, Mr. Smith, and give it a try, but to tell you the truth, I'm not sure how far I would get. You seem to have covered most everything yourself. From what you say, she hasn't left any clues, and since she's been up and down the Eastern Seaboard over the past few years, picking a city to go looking for her would be like shooting craps. I'd suggest that you sit still for a while—"

"I can't do that! I need to find her!"

Adept at dealing with frantic clients, the man gestured consolingly and spoke with utter calm. "You will. You will, in time. It's been my experience that something eventually turns up. For example, she's going to have to contact her landlady about retrieving the things in her apartment. The woman said she'd let you know?"

"Yes. But that could take weeks."

"You may just have to wait. There's also the postmaster. A woman starting out in a new city is going to need every penny she can get."

"You don't know Pepper," John muttered, convinced that she could live on peanuts if she so chose.

"Nonetheless, at some point she will contact him. You'll see. It'll just take patience on your part. If you'd like me to come in at that point—or at any other point when you have more to go on—just give me a call."

John thanked him and left, feeling utterly despondent during the drive back to Naples. He just didn't know where to go, where to look. He'd exhausted every possibility. If only she had family. She did! A father and a brother! He stepped on the gas and headed for the library.

Pam was more than willing to take a break to talk with him. They went out into the lawn behind the building.

"Did she ever say much about her father?" he asked, tempering eagerness with a certain caution.

"Just that he'd left when she was seven and that she'd been hurt badly."

"Mmm. That's what she told me. But do you have any idea where he lives? I know that she was born somewhere here in Maine."

"But they moved away before she was three—"

"To New Jersey. Then her father and brother took off four years later and she never saw them again—"

"Which is why it'd be useless to try to track them down," Pam argued gently. As much as she wanted John to find Pepper, she hated to see him cling to false hopes. "Pepper wouldn't go to them, even if she knew where to find them."

"What if, just supposing, they kept tabs on *her*."

"Without her knowing?"

"There's always that possibility."

"But her father was the one who left without looking back."

"Now we don't know that, do we? We don't know what caused the split. For all we know, her mother ordered them out. For all we know, her father may have suffered greatly, may have loved his daughter all these years—"

"If that were true, he would have gone to her when her mother died!"

Then John sat back. "You've got a point," he murmured pensively. "Still, there's always a chance."

"If Pepper's escaped us, she would have escaped him, too."

"Pam, I don't know where else to look. Even on the most remote chance that he may know something we don't, I have to try to find him. But that could be a major problem in itself." The wheels were turning, but they badly needed grease. "It's improbable that he would have stayed in Jersey."

"They could have gone anywhere."

"But if they had roots up here, it's possible they returned. Do you know what he did for a living?"

"No. Pepper never said."

"Did she ever mention grandparents?"

"Not on her father's side. For that matter, not on her mother's, either. There were—"

"The cousins who took her in when her mother died. Do you know their name?"

Pam shook her head. "It wouldn't be MacNeil."

"No." John pondered the next step. "But somewhere, on one of those job applications.... Wait." His eyes widened as inspiration hit. "Vassar."

Pam grinned. "I think you may have something there."

"Right. Well, listen, I gotta go." He put both hands on Pam's shoulders, then on impulse bent to kiss her cheek. "You've been an angel!"

"I didn't do anything!" she protested, but he was already halfway across the lawn.

"You did," he called back. "You listened!"

"Will you let me know if you learn anything?" she yelled, as concerned about Pepper as she was about the man who seemed to be so desperate without her.

"Sure thing!" he promised moments before he disappeared into the parking lot.

Indeed, he did learn the names of the New Jersey relatives with whom Pepper had spent her teenage years. He called them. Unfortunately, they thought she was still in Philadelphia. It had been nearly four years since they'd last heard from her. Regarding her father, they had no idea of his whereabouts, though they acknowledged that he'd originally been from Maine.

Late that night, sitting alone on his porch in the dark, with only the crickets to ward off total silence, John worked with the pieces of the puzzle, shifting them, rearranging them, until at last they began to fit. When Pepper had graduated from school, she'd taken a job in Atlanta. Then she'd moved to Bethesda, then Philadelphia, then Boston...then Naples. Steadily north. Steadily back toward the place where she'd been born.

The next morning he went in search of Pepper's birth certificate. If he had to shoot in the dark, it was far easier working county by county than town by town. He began with Cumberland County, in which Naples was located, but found nothing in the county files by way of a birth certificate. He drove farther north into Oxford County and met similar results. It was above that, in Franklin County, that he hit paydirt.

Pepper's father's name was Andrew. He and his wife had been living in Rangeley when she'd been born. Packing an overnight bag, John headed north on Friday morning, intent on spending as many days as it might take to scour the town for word of one Andrew Mac-Neil.

He didn't have to go far. The local chief of police recognized the name instantly as that of a schoolmate of his many years before. He said that Andrew MacNeil was now living in Stratton, just a bit up the road.

The Scout ate up the distance in no time flat. Nearing the small town center, John pulled over at a gas station and flipped through the local phone book until he found the proper entry. The station attendant gave him directions to the address listed, and John soon found himself on a private road, at the end of which was sprawled no less than six clusters of modern condominiums. It wasn't quite what John had expected, though in truth he didn't know what to expect. He was about to meet the man who had hurt Pepper so long ago. He might feel like spitting in his eye, but the man might have the information he needed.

Finding number 304, appropriately the fourth home in the third cluster, he rang the bell. No one answered. But it was the middle of the afternoon, he reasoned. Andrew MacNeil might well be at work, wherever that was.

He rang the bell a second time, just to be sure, then turned to find that one of the residents of a neighboring home had come out.

"Are you looking for Andrew?"

"That's right. It's very important that I talk with him."

"He's away. Down in Boston. Won't be back till the first of the week."

John let out a deep sigh of frustration. Another door temporarily shut. He didn't want to wait that long—but did he have a choice?

Resigning himself, he thanked the neighbor and left. Had this been New York, he realized, he would have learned nothing. Wariness would probably have prevented the man from speaking. But it wasn't New York and he did have Andrew MacNeil's phone number. He'd start calling on Monday.

That was what he did, but it wasn't until Tuesday evening that the phone was finally answered.

"Hello?" a deep, gravelly voice said.

"Andrew MacNeil, please."

"Speaking."

"Uh, Mr. MacNeil, my name is John Smith. I'm calling about your daughter." He held his breath.

There was a lengthy pause at the other end of the line. "I have no daughter. You must have the wrong number."

"No. Please. I'm sure I don't—"

He was interrupted by a click. Andrew MacNeil had hung up. John quickly dialed again. The phone rang a full eight times before the man answered. His "hello" was slightly gruff. John started right in.

"Please don't hang up, Mr. MacNeil. My situation is urgent. You don't have to say anything. Just hear me out." The silence on the other end encouraged him; it was better than nothing. "I'm the head of the guidance department at the Lake Region High School, but that's got little to do with Pepper. I just want you to know that I'm on the level. You can check me out, if you wish. The school will vouch for my legitimacy. I'm not trying to hurt you, I simply want to locate Pepper." He ventured a hesitant, "Are you there?"

"Yes." Begrudgingly perhaps, but there nonetheless.

John was instantly relieved; at least the man was listening. "I met Pepper last month; she is—was—the mailman in Naples, where I live. We grew very close and, well, I love her, and I believe she loves me. But she's frightened of admitting it." He took a deep breath and forced himself to go on. "She left over a week ago, Mr. MacNeil. Very suddenly. She's been doing that for a long time, I gather, running from place to place to avoid making attachments. She's spent time in many cities all along the Eastern Seaboard, but she's been moving steadily northward, I'm sure because she was born up here.

"I need to find her. For her sake, as well as for mine. I've done everything I can to locate her, but I'm running into dead ends. I thought, well, there was a remote possibility that she might try to contact you or your son." He paused then, waiting. When there was no response on the other end of the line, he realized that Andrew MacNeil would be little help. John's voice held a note of defeat when he spoke again.

"I'd like to give you my address and phone number. If you hear anything, anything at all, I'd greatly appreciate your calling me." Very slowly, he dictated the information, praying that the man was humane enough to take it down. Then he spoke very quietly. "Thank you. I want you to know.... I want you to know that your daughter is a very special person. She's intelligent and witty and charming and caring." His voice cracked, but he forced himself to continue. "I love her deeply. A future without her would be meaningless." He'd said it all. He clutched the phone tightly, waiting. It was Andrew MacNeil's turn to speak. The silence seemed endless. At long last it was broken.

"I have no daughter," was all the man said before he hung up the phone. But it was enough. John heard the slight tremor that made a lie of his words. Oh, he had a daughter, all right. Had he not, he never would have sat listening to John pour out his heart. He would have hung up at the start, perhaps after threatening to call the telephone company or the police.

John felt no measure of victory, though. He'd learned nothing. If Andrew MacNeil did, indeed, have information on Pepper's whereabouts, he'd chosen not to share it. All John could do was hope that he might have a change of heart in time.

TIME. IT PASSED at a snail's pace for John during the next week, though he tried to keep busy finishing up work on the house. Each day without fail he visited the postmaster, then Pepper's landlady, but neither one heard a word from Pepper. Pam called him every so often, as did Jenna. His neighbors on Casey Lane made special trips to his house to ask if he'd heard anything from her. But he hadn't. He was totally discouraged.

School began with a spate of faculty meetings. He attended them all, even managed to look attentive and pleased, when in truth his heart was elsewhere. When the students arrived, his day was more demanding. But the nights, the nights were quiet and lonely.

He thought about Pepper constantly. She was a silent presence in his life. When he reached for her, though, his hands grasped air. He wondered how long he'd have to suffer for the dubious crime of loving her.

Classes were in their second week when, on a Tuesday evening, he received a telephone call. As always, he jumped, daring to hope that it might be Pepper. At the sound of the male voice at the other end of the line, his hopes fell, only to soar again when he recognized the distinct gravelly tone.

"Mr. Smith," the voice began, slightly unsure, "this is Andrew MacNeil."

"Mr. MacNeil! Thank you for calling! Have you heard something?"

"I . . . not really. I just thought you ought to know that someone's been asking about me."

"Someone there?"

"No. There have been . . . phone calls . . . to the town halls, both in Rangeley and Stratton. I know...many of the people. The clerk from Stratton called me."

"Did she say if it was a woman calling?"

"It was."

John's head started to thud. "A local call?"

"Long distance, she thought."

"The caller didn't identify herself?"

"No."

"What did she want to know?"

"She wanted to know whether there was an Andrew MacNeil living in town." He cleared his throat, obviously feeling awkward. "It may be nothing. But I thought you'd want to know."

"I do! There's been no word at all down here. At least if it was Pepper asking about you, we know that she's thinking clearly." He wanted to elaborate, to say that she was seeking out her father for a reason, but he wasn't sure how much the other man could take. "It seems that all I can do is to wait. There are times when I think I'll lose my mind...." He realized he was babbling. "Well, anyway, thank you, Mr. MacNeil. I do appreciate your call—"

"Uh, Mr. Smith?"

"Yes?"

"You'll ... you'll let me know ... if you find her?"

It was as close as he had come to admitting that Pepper was his daughter. John felt instantly heartened. "Of course. Thank you."

Sitting back on the sofa in the den after hanging up the phone, John realized that the man didn't seem as bad as he might have been given the little he knew about him. He also realized that he was no closer to learning where Pepper was.

Closing his eyes, he tried to picture her as she might be at that moment. He wondered what she was wearing, where she'd been that day, what she'd had for dinner, whether she had just taken a long, jasmine-rich bath. He wondered if she'd remembered to get her allergy shot; it had been more than four weeks since her last—

Bolting upright, he grasped the edge of the sofa. Instants later he was running up the winding stairs, dashing into his bedroom, shoving miscellaneous cards and cuff links around the small leather box atop his dresser, in search of the small piece of paper that bore the name of the doctor who'd treated her when she'd been stung.

Hands trembling, he found it, then ran to the phone. He should have *thought*. It was a long shot that the man would be on duty. But, then, John was becoming accustomed to failure when it came to locating Pepper. He had nothing to lose. If not tonight, he'd reach the doctor tomorrow.

"Dr. Manley, please," he gasped when the switchboard operator at the hospital answered. "It's urgent."

"I'm sorry, the offices are closed for the day. I can leave a message with his answering service—"

"Would you try the Emergency Room? He may be there."

"One minute, please."

Moments later John was repeating his request to the nurse at the Emergency Room desk. Again he was put on hold. He knew his luck had finally turned when the doctor came on the line.

"Dr. Manley, this is John Smith. I was there at the hospital about five weeks ago with Pepper MacNeil when she had a severe reaction to a bee sting. We were back a week later for an allergy shot?"

"Yes, Mr. Smith. I do remember."

"Uh, I'm trying to locate Pepper." As succinctly as possible, he outlined the situation. Then he made his bid.

"Is it possible that someone called for her records? If she's gone for a shot in another city, that doctor may have wanted them."

"I didn't get a call. I'm sure of it. But that doesn't mean one didn't come in or that the records weren't sent. I could check, if you'd like to hold."

"Very much," John answered. He knew he was on to something. Pepper was too responsible to skip her allergy shot. *Why hadn't he thought of it sooner?*

"You're in luck, Mr. Smith, although I'm not sure I should be divulging this information. You're not family."

"I will be. Please. I need to reach her."

His quiet plea was enough to overcome the doctor's hesitancy. "We received a request from a small clinic in...uh, Newport, Vermont. A Dr. Slater is handling the case." He proceeded to give John the name of the clinic.

With profuse thank-yous, John pressed the cutoff button, then dialed Information. As he suspected, the clinic was closed for the night. He debated leaving an urgent message with the answering service but realized that if he'd waited this long, he could wait a few more hours. He doubted the doctor would have Pepper's address at home with him anyway. Besides, there was a kind of satisfaction simply in having tracked Pepper this far. He wanted—he *needed*—a few hours to dream that he might actually see her soon. If the doctor had bad news for him tomorrow, if she'd taken her shot and run, he didn't want to know till morning. He was so close, so close! Every one of his senses came alive.

Feeling more energetic than he had in days, he dug out a map of New England to find that Newport was very near the Canadian border. She hadn't strayed far; that said something else. She might have gone to the deep South or the Midwest, but she'd stayed in New England. To be near her father . . . or him?

If loneliness and worry had kept him awake for long hours during the past weeks, tonight it was anticipation. Come morning, he dressed and headed for school. He'd already met separately with two students and a parent when nine o'clock finally arrived.

He dialed the clinic, then waited, rubbing his forehead, until the receptionist came on the line. When she announced that the doctor was tied up with a patient, he explained his dilemma, offering, as he had to Andrew MacNeil, his credentials as proof of his character. Certain information was privileged; he had to make these people understand how urgent the situation was.

After listening patiently, the woman asked if he could call back in an hour. She had to check with the doctor, she explained, then, if he agreed to pass on Pepper's address, she had to find it in the files. John wanted to ask how difficult that would be in such a small-town clinic, but he knew that sarcasm would do more harm than good. He held his tongue and agreed to call back.

It was actually a full ninety minutes before he was able to do so. He'd had a class, then another conference. By the time he returned to his office, he was damp around the collar.

This time, when he identified himself, the doctor came on the line. "We don't usually do this," he explained, "but the woman does seem to be all alone. And your credentials check out."

John ignored the last. "Is she all right?"

"She's fine. Tired perhaps, and a bit rundown. I gave her the allergy shot and prescribed some vitamins."

"Is she working?"

"She's conducting tours at one of the historic buildings in town. We're so close to the border that we get French-speaking people here all the time. It's an asset, her being bilingual."

John had to smile. "She's a marvel.... Uh, you do have her address?"

"Oh, yes." He read it off while John wrote it down, then asked, "Will you be coming up?"

"Tomorrow, so help me, tomorrow."

PEPPER PACKED the last of her clothes in her suitcase and took a final look around the small room she'd called home for the past few weeks. As boardinghouses went, it was a notch above, but it was nothing compared to her garage apartment in Naples...or John's beautiful home.

She was going back. The decision had come slowly and she was more nervous than she would have imagined. There was the distinct possibility that John wouldn't want her, that he'd been angered so much by her flight that whatever he'd felt for her had died. She prayed that wasn't the case.

She loved him. Even now, saying the words, she was afraid. But she couldn't deny them any longer. Life without him—even in spite of this job, which was challenging and fun—was no life at all.

It was time to stop running. She was finally willing to take the chance that, loving John and having that love returned, she might find the happiness she'd glimpsed that summer. If it didn't last, it didn't last. But she simply couldn't turn her back on something she'd wanted for so very long.

Chin up, she lifted the suitcase, scanned the room for anything she might have left, then went downstairs to her car. She'd given notice to her employer but had agreed to work this final day before leaving. By late afternoon she'd be on her way. By night she'd be back in Naples. By morning . . . by morning she might be in John's arms, if he still wanted her. . . .

IT WASN'T UNTIL NOON that John reached the address Dr. Slater had given him. He wasn't sure if Pepper would be working, but since he didn't have her work address, he'd had no choice as to where to start.

When he didn't see her car in the driveway of the large white house, his heart sank. But the house was far too big for Pepper to have lived there alone, and his hopes revived. Someone was home; the front door was open.

Leaving the Scout at the curb, he trotted up the front walk and took the steps two at a time. A short knock was all it took for a sprightly senior citizen to appear.

"Mornin'," the man said.

"Good morning," John returned, trying to sound amiable when in fact his insides were knotted up. "I'm looking for Pepper MacNeil. I was told she lived here."

"She did. But she's gone."

Gone. He felt a familiar sense of dread. Could it have happened again? Was he too late?

"You mean," he returned optimistically, "that she's at work."

"That too. She signed out this morning. I'm gonna miss her. She was one of the nicest boarders I've had in years."

Bidden by urgency, John gripped the edge of the open screen door. "Ah, look, I've come a long way to see her. Could you tell me where she works?"

"Sure." He pointed down the street. "Go that way till you reach a fork, then go right. Can't miss it. Big brick house on the left with a fancy shingle out front. Only one on the street."

"Thank you," John called. He was already down the stairs. "I appreciate it."

It took him less than five minutes to reach the brick house the man had indicated. It took far longer for him to decide what to do. He sat in the Scout, staring at the familiar Rabbit parked in the small lot beside the house. His hands gripped the steering wheel with such ferocity that it was a miracle they didn't leave marks when finally he loosened his hold.

He couldn't believe he'd found her, but he had. She was here. If the man at the boardinghouse had been correct, though, she wouldn't be much longer. He wondered where her next stop would be and experienced the same rising anger that had stalked him for so many days after her departure from Naples. In time, supplanted by concern, longing and love, the anger had receded. But it was back now in force. His clenched jaw was rock hard. Pepper had run once too often, he decided; she was about to pay the piper.

Slamming out of the Scout, he stormed up the walk of the venerable brick house, yanked the door open and entered. The front hall was dim, lit only indirectly by the tall windows in adjoining rooms. It took him a minute to realize that a fragile-looking young woman sat at a nearby desk, eyeing him with something akin to fear. He did nothing to soften his glower.

"Is Pepper MacNeil here?" he demanded.

"Y-yes. But she's in the middle of a tour."

"Where are they?" Hearing the softest murmur from one of the upstairs rooms, he started up the stairs.

"Sir, you can't—"

Ignoring her, he reached the landing, then looked around and followed the voice. Pepper was in the largest of the upstairs rooms, which had been exquisitely restored in early American style. A small group of people formed a loose circle before her. John stood straight and tall at the door, his arms crossed over his chest. One part of him melted at the sight of her looking so pretty, so utterly feminine in a broad-bibbed blouse and an ankle-length ruffled skirt, her voice as sweet and lyrical as a nightingale from France. The other part of him hurt and boiled and determined that she wouldn't escape him this time.

She'd been looking at the rolltop desk she'd been describing for the tourists. When she turned and caught sight of John, her voice broke midsentence. She was overjoyed to see him, elated to think he'd gone to the effort of tracking her down. But all she could focus on at the moment was his obvious fury.

The color drained from her face. She swallowed hard, then continued to speak. But the flow of her words was less smooth. Several faces turned toward John, eyes speculating on the effect this imposing man's appearance had had on their previously unruffled tour guide. John, in turn, felt a perverse kind of satisfaction at having shaken Pepper. She deserved it, he mused. She deserved far more!

Pepper didn't know how she went on. She could barely remember the lines she'd so completely memorized for the tour, and stumbled more than once. John looked livid. He hated her! She'd blown it!

Speaking softly in French, she indicated that the group should move on to the next room. When they turned and began to file past John, who'd moved aside only slightly, she felt her composure slip. Tears gathered at her lower lids. She put her head down and took a deep breath, trying to restore her calm. The show must go on, she reminded herself, then swallowed hard when it came her turn to follow the last of her charges from the room.

John stepped in front of her, barring her way. "What time are you done?" he demanded, his tone as threatening as his expression.

"I, uh, I finish this tour in ten minutes." Her voice sounded foreign, shaky and unsure. "I lead another one at three."

"Can you get out of it?"

"I don't know."

"Do it," he ordered, only then stepping back so she could proceed. But he followed her, determined not to let her out of his sight for a minute. He didn't trust her. She was inventive. She'd find some way to sneak off if he let her. And he had no intention of doing that, not now, not ever.

The next ten minutes were pure hell for Pepper. Every hope she'd had of returning to John, of declaring her love, of finding that love returned, was dashed. The inner pain she felt was even greater than that she'd experienced when she'd left him.

After what seemed an eternity of anguish, the tour group returned to the lower front hall and disbanded with a quiet *"Merci"* to Pepper and an occasional curious glance at John.

"Let's go," he stated, taking Pepper's elbow in an iron grip when the last of the tourists had cleared the front door.

"I, uh. . . ." She was about to remind him that she had another tour to lead, but his expression was so lacking in understanding that she lost her customary nerve. For that matter, she realized, she'd lost much of what had been customary to her nature. Loving John, leaving him, now losing him was having an irrevocable effect on her life. "Just a minute," she whispered, forcing an apologetic smile toward the woman behind the desk. She turned toward the back of the house, but John tightened his grip on her elbow.

"Oh, no, you don't. No sneaking off this time."

"I have to speak with my boss," she murmured, knowing she deserved John's accusation but feeling a hint of irritation. He didn't have to show up to tell her that he didn't want her. He could have simply stayed in Naples and courted someone else. She'd have learned soon enough when she returned that he was no longer interested. So much for the power of love! She'd been right all along.

It occurred to her as she walked down the hall with John closely in tow that there was now no need for her to leave Newport. She had a place to live—she was sure her room would be free if she decided to stay—and a rewarding job. But then there were her belongings in Naples; she might as well get them. And as of today, there would be memories here—of John's anger, his disdain—that she knew would haunt her. No, she'd leave and find some other place, one with no memories, to rebuild a life. As for finally seeing her father, well, he didn't want that anyway. She'd been planning it for her own sake, to try to understand what had happened so many years ago.

She spoke quietly with the woman in the small office at the end of the hall and was assured that, though she'd miss her, the younger woman at the desk could lead the afternoon's tour since she'd be taking over the next day anyway. She gave Pepper the money owed her, then wished her luck, not realizing how badly Pepper might need luck in the long, lonely nights ahead.

Only after Pepper had led the way to the street did she turn to face John. Her knees were shaky, but she willed them to hold her steady.

"All right, John. What do you want?"

His eyes were like charcoal, dark and hard. "You're coming back with me." He took her arm and propelled her toward the Scout.

"No! I've got my own car—"

"Uh-uh. Not this time. You're too slick."

"I can't leave it here!" She knew she'd need it when she packed up her things in Naples and rented a trailer. "I'm not coming back."

"Oh, you're coming back all right—"

"Not to Newport. I was planning to leave anyway."

"I know," he growled, but relented only when inspiration hit. Abruptly changing direction, he ushered her to the Rabbit. "Give me your wallet. And the check you just got."

"What?"

"You're going to be directly in front of me all the way back to Naples. I'll hold the driver's license and every cent you've got. If you try to lose me, you'll be without money for gas or food or lodging."

"I don't believe you," she whispered. He truly did distrust her. It hurt fiercely. She lowered her eyes so he couldn't see her pain. Along with everything else, she felt humiliated. "I won't try to lose you—"

"I'm not taking that chance." He held out a hand. "Your wallet? Make that the entire purse. Who knows what you might have stuffed in a side pocket." Anxious only to see this horror scene over, she did as he asked. "Get in the car," he stated more quietly. Again she acquiesced, flinching when the door slammed shut by her side. He leaned low at the open window. "I think you know the way. I'll be right behind you." Then he was gone, striding toward the Scout.

Pepper started her engine and backed around, then left the parking lot and headed down the road. The Scout was a large white tail behind her. She started to laugh at the image of the cottontail rabbit, but the laugh broke apart and she bit her lip to keep from crying.

Unfortunately, her emotions were too raw to be contained. She drove for five minutes, then ten, blinking furiously, swallowing convulsively in an attempt to dislodge the hard knot in her throat. It was a losing battle. When she could no longer see the road through her tears, she pulled over to the side and put on the brake. Then, head hung low, arms draped weakly over the steering wheel, she began to cry freely.

John was at her window in the seconds it took him to park behind her and storm from his car. "Pepper, I told you to drive! Can't you even follow the simplest direc—" The sight of her hunched shoulders, her tear-streaked cheeks stemmed his words. But much as his heart was breaking in two, he refused to be affected by

her tears. Opening her door, he spoke wearily. "Get out."
When she seemed unable to move, he helped her, propping her against the side of the car, then stepping back
with his hands on his hips. He'd been determined to save
the confrontation until they were back in the privacy of
his house, but somehow, where Pepper was concerned,
nothing went as planned.

9

"LOOK," HE BEGAN, "this is hard for both of us, but I think your childishness has gone far enough. You can only run so long. I won't let you do it again. That was the dumbest thing I've ever seen, taking off the way you did! And leaving this crummy note?" He pulled out the badly rumpled letter, worn at the edges from constant transfer from one pair of pants to the next, and waved it before her nose. "What kind of stupidity was that?"

His voice jumped an octave in mime of her voice; he knew the words by heart: "Why not give either Pamela Hoffman or Jenna Lloyd a call." His voice returned to its normal deep pitch as he continued. "Oh, yeah, I called them, all right. Called them to help me find you. They've been pretty upset, too, but, no, you didn't think of that when you packed up your bags and took the coward's way out. You're right. You *are* a coward. Dammit, Pepper, look at me!" She'd been slouched against the car with her head bowed, crying softly. "And stop that damned sobbing!" He whipped a hand through his hair. "I can't take it. You know that."

It was the first indication Pepper had had that any softness remained in John. She didn't know whether to be hopeful or simply grateful. Either way, there was too much she wanted to say for her to stay silent. Though her chin remained glued to her chest, she began to speak. "I was afraid, so afraid . . . I refused to admit . . . to myself that I loved you and . . . then when I met your family and . . . they were everything I'd always wanted . . . I couldn't handle it anymore." She paused to wipe her cheeks. When her fingers came away wet, she pressed them to her skirt. "I was so worried that it'd all . . . end up to be nothing more than a dream because . . . I wanted it so badly that. . . ." She couldn't go on. Her knees began to buckle, but she'd only slid an inch down the side of the car before John caught her. Holding her arms, he used his own body to prop her against the car.

"What are you saying?" He asked in the voice she knew so well, a voice filled with need.

It took her a minute before she could stop crying and raise her eyes. "I love you," she whispered, "and I know I made a mistake."

"But you were leaving here . . ." John began, almost afraid to believe what he was hearing.

"To come back to you," she asserted more forcefully. Her tears began to flow all the faster. "I wasn't . . . sure if you'd have me but I had to . . . to take that chance. My life has been hell since I . . . left. I can't sleep. I can't eat. I . . . it's so lonely all the time and I . . . exist only for the . . . memories of what we had. . . ."

A deep moan, a hybrid of pain, relief and joy, emerged from John's throat instants before he hauled her against him and secured her tightly in his arms. "Oh, sweetheart, you don't know what it means to me to hear you say that." His voice was rough in a ragged but gentle way.

Stunned, Pepper looked up at him and saw that his own eyes were brilliant, sparkling with moisture.

"Oh, no, John, don't do that!" she gasped, reaching up to brush at the lone tear that trickled to his cheek. "You're so strong. I've always needed that!"

John had no intention of apologizing. "Strong men often cry, especially when they hurt as much as I have since you've been gone."

"Then you . . . still love me?" Pepper asked, afraid to believe.

"I'll love you forever. Nothing you ever do can change that. Which is one of the reasons it was so dumb of you to suggest that I see either Pam or Jenna. I agree with you; they're both wonderful. But I doubt that either of them would want the shell I was without you, or the fact that they'd be involved with a man who was forever in love with a ghost."

"I'm not a ghost."

"Are you sure?" He moved his hands to her neck, then her face, needing to feel the reality of the features he adored so.

"I'm sure," she whispered, ready to burst with the joy that had so suddenly emerged from the darkest pit of despair. Her own hands found his waist, then slid open-palmed up his back as though to reassure herself that he, too, was there. By the time her fingers reached his shoulders, she was on tiptoe, lips seeking his.

He met her halfway with a kiss that was so forceful, so resonant with love, that it was a good thing when, arms wrapped around her, he lifted her off her feet. Her legs never would have held her.

How long they stood there, lips devouring lips, tongues, hands, bodies reacquainting, they didn't know. The occasional car passed them but they were oblivious to everything but the wonder of each other. It was only when one of those cars pulled up and its door slammed that they looked up. Forced from a land where love ruled all, it took them a minute to realize it was a policeman who swaggered forward.

"Okay, folks. Times up. You're gonna have to find some other place for this. We're gonna have an accident pretty soon when traffic picks up and nobody watches the road for watching you two."

Taking a shuddering breath, John straightened. He cleared his throat. "Sorry, officer. I'm afraid we got carried away."

"That's okay. Just so long as you get movin'. And pick up that litter, will you?" He shot a meaningful glance at the crumpled letter, Pepper's letter, which John had unknowingly dropped. "There's a fine for that kind of thing," he called over his shoulder as he ambled back to his car.

John knelt to retrieve the letter while Pepper struggled to temper the desire that continued to shoot through her veins. He stuffed it back in his pocket with a grin.

"Don't want to lose this."

"Throw it out, John. I'm so ashamed—"

"No way. I think I'll have it framed as a reminder of past transgressions." When her pained look continued, he came closer, pressing her to the car. "You weren't the only one at fault, Pepper. I was blind, too. I should have known what you were thinking, should have forced you to talk about it." His body strained toward hers, subtly finding its fit against her slender curves. "I'm supposed to be attuned to emotions, but my own really muddied up my thinking about yours."

His voice was so soft, so caring that Pepper gave up the battle against her clamoring senses. Unaware of what she was doing, she bent her right leg to rub the back of her left knee.

"John . . . I don't know . . . do you think there's a motel on this road?"

The policeman honked in passing and John stepped quickly away from her, pasting a patronizing smile on his face and waving to the disappearing cruiser. When he looked back at Pepper, his smile had become a mock-lascivious grin that sizzled its way through her, not helping her dilemma a bit. It took her only a minute to realize that the dilemma was his as well.

He cast a glance down the road, then beyond the car toward where a thick stand of birch trees stood. "Come on," he said, taking her hand and pulling her around the car toward the trees.

"John! Not here! We can't—"

"Why not?" They'd entered the woods. He led her farther.

"He'll come back. Then we'll really be in trouble."

"The way I see it," John drawled, drawing her onward until the road was barely visible, "we'll be in trouble trying to drive in a state of such...dubious control." He'd come to rest with his back braced against the sheltered side of a broad fir. The road was well behind them. He twirled Pepper into his arms. "Besides, your skirt will hide a multitude of sins. Have I told you how pretty you look?"

"No," she whispered, meeting his lips, kissing him with the hunger that had only been momentarily appeased at the car. His tongue delved into her depths, then he moaned and licked the side of her mouth. His hands were on the buckle of his belt.

She heard the rasp of his zipper as he whispered, "Just slip your panties off. It'll be okay. You'll see."

She wasn't so sure, but at that moment, she didn't care if they were hauled off for lewd and lascivious conduct in a public place. The trees were their shroud, the love they shared was their defense.

"We could always plead temporary insanity," she gasped, reaching under her skirt to do as John had said. When her panties hit the ground, John put his arms around her waist and slid down, his back braced against the tree. Tugging her skirt from beneath her, he eased her thighs around his hips. Then, needing no preliminaries, he was inside her, hard and throbbing, filling her with the greatest joy she could imagine.

She cried his name, then bit her lip as the heat burst within. His hands remained under her skirt, guiding her hips, caressing the soft flesh of her bottom.

"Temporary insanity...wouldn't do," he grunted as he thrust up hard. "You know as well as I do—" he re-

treated, then arched again "—that there's . . . nothing
temporary about this . . . ahhh."

Pepper rode him with abandon. She felt wild, exhilarated and so filled with love that seconds later, when her
body quivered, then tensed, then exploded, she was sure
John would have to pick the tiny fragments of herself
from the forest floor to encase with her letter as a me-
mento of the woman who'd died of sheer, unadulterated
bliss. It was only when John gave a final, deep thrust and
reached his own shattering climax that she realized she
was whole, more whole than she'd been in her life.

He sensed it, too. "Do you know what that felt like?"
he asked, panting. His eyes were closed, his forehead
resting against hers. She shook her head, loving the way
he smelled when passion filled his pores. "It felt suddenly like . . . I was twice the person I'd ever been. No, it
was as if I didn't exist anymore as a separate being. . . ."
He didn't talk then, but, savoring the aftermath of total
unity, waited until his breathing finally eased. Then he
chuckled. "I'd congratulate myself on my speed except
that you came before I did."

"I think we should congratulate each other," she murmured in his ear, "although I kind of missed touching
your chest and your nipples, your stomach and your—"

"Geez, Pepper, cut it out! *Your* bare ass isn't on pine
needles." He arched his hips and she suspected it was to
have a final feel of her before he eased her off him. "I can
think of more comfortable places to make love." His
voice softened and he took her face tenderly in his hands.
"But none as meaningful as this spot. Next time some-

thing's wrong, let's try to see the forest through the trees, hmmm?"

She smiled. "Mmmm."

"Wanna go home?"

"Oh, yes."

He pulled her to her feet and they both repaired their clothing. Then, arm in arm, they returned to the road.

VERY, VERY LATE that night they lay in John's big bed, warm and replete in the aftermath of passion. For as fast as their lovemaking had been in the Vermont woods that afternoon, this time it had been magnificently slow. John had worshipped every inch of her body, speaking of his love in ways that might have made Pepper blush had she not been reciprocating the declaration with as intimate an appreciation.

"You have a fantastic body," she breathed. "I love the way you taste . . . everywhere."

"The feeling is mutual, I can assure you."

"John," she said abruptly, "I want to have a baby."

"You do." There was pleasure in his brief response.

She pushed herself up and rested her forearms on his chest. Sexual teasing was forgotten. "Yes. I wanted it before, when I was trying to deny that I loved you. If I'd gotten pregnant then, I would have used it as an excuse to stay with you. Do you know what I'm saying? I would have been able to stay even *without* admitting that I loved you." Her eyes lowered. "When I found I wasn't pregnant, and when, well, your family came and all, I guess I panicked. My ace in the hole was gone; it was like I had to lay my cards on the table, but I just couldn't."

"Don't you realize," John said, tenderly stroking her hair away from her face, "that the cards in your hand were every bit as high, if not higher than the ace? Don't mistake me, sweetheart. I want children, too. Very badly. But if they never come I could be more than content to simply have you for the rest of my life."

"Do you think there's . . . any problem?"

"With what?"

"My . . . ability to conceive?"

"Are you kidding? Sweetheart, couples sometimes work for years to make a baby. We've been at it, what, a month? Of course there's nothing wrong. As long as we keep it up—"

Pepper's kiss absorbed the rest of his words. When at last she snuggled back into the crook of his shoulder, it was with the softest of sighs. "I don't think I've ever been so happy. It was so lonely up there without you."

"I think you enjoyed your job, though."

"I did. It was fun. Nice people. But then, all of my jobs have been that way." She laughed, her breath ruffling the soft hair on his chest. "The people here are so great. Did you see the way they all came out when we drove down the street?"

"They missed you. It nearly drove me crazy. They used to come down here asking about you and I'd feel so frustrated because I didn't know anything myself. I'd get all angry inside because it was like they were making it worse, when in fact they were only expressing concern.

It's a good thing I found you. Much more and I would have been screeching at them like a raving lunatic. I think we should give a barbecue for them all. They really were supportive."

Pepper nodded her agreement against his breast, then turned the gesture into a head shake of amazement. "You're quite a sleuth, John Smith." He'd explained how he'd finally tracked her down. "I think you're in the wrong line of work—oh, John!" She jumped up again. "I haven't asked! Tell me about school!"

He grinned and pulled her down again. "School's fine. At least, I think it will be now. I've been slightly distracted."

"You didn't work today!"

"Obviously."

"It didn't even occur to me until now, I'm so used to your being free. You had to miss school for me. I'm sorry."

"I'm not. It was worth it. Which is not to say that I dare play hooky tomorrow. *One* of us needs to work."

"That's right. I am unemployed. You say there's a new carrier?"

"Uh-huh. Another lady."

"Is she pretty?"

"If you like Mack trucks."

"Oh. That's unkind, John."

He shrugged. "Would you rather I'd have said, 'Yes, she's pretty'?"

"No."

"Okay. Now that we've got that settled, let's get back to the subject of your employment. You don't have to work at all, y'know."

"I do. I'd go crazy with you at school all day. Besides, I've never been a freeloader."

"You mean you wouldn't want to be—" he lowered his voice to a mischievous drawl "—a kept woman?" When Pepper tugged hard at the hair on his chest, he protested. "Easy does it. That stuff was hard earned. So, what would you like to do?"

"I dunno," she said, stroking that part of him she'd just injured. "I kind of enjoyed conducting my tours."

"I'm not sure there are any historical buildings offering tours around here, and if there were, the tours would be in English."

She propped her chin on his chest and looked smugly up at him. "Then I'll have to find someplace around here where French *is* spoken."

He frowned. "None of the shops need interpreters, and the businesses are too small to be able to afford one. You could always do translation work here at the house—you know, correspond with academicians in Boston and New York. No," he said, pondering the dilemma, "you like to be with people." His eyes lit up. "I know! You could tutor. There are French courses taught at the high school. I'm sure there'd be work, maybe even for occasional subbing, maybe even for a course of your own at some point." His voice rose with each successive "maybe."

His expression brimmed with such open enthusiasm that Pepper burst into a gale of laughter. "You should see your eyes! Such . . . such unpretentious innocence!"

"But what do you think of my idea? It's brilliant, if I do say so myself."

"I think it's brilliant, too. I have from the moment it came to me last week."

"Last week. Oh." He grimaced in a sheepish way. "Well, whose ever idea it is or was, it's a good one. Want me to check with the head of the French department tomorrow?"

"No, *I'll* check with the head of the French department, but not tomorrow. I . . . need a little time."

Hearing something unsettling in her voice, John brought his head up from the pillow. "Pepper, you are going to marry me, aren't you?"

"Yes." She smiled. "I'm going to marry you."

"When?"

She took a deep breath. "As soon as I see my father."

"Your father."

"Yes."

John was suddenly hesitant. He knew she had to do it, knew she had to finally work things out in her mind, knew what courage it took for her to finally realize it. But he also knew that she could be in for a disappointment. All too well he remembered Andrew MacNeil's twice repeated, "I have no daughter." And despite the call John had received the other night, he was skeptical. He didn't want her to be hurt. He was frightened himself, frightened that a meeting between father and daughter, if emotionally unsatisfactory, might do something to re-vive her fear of commitment. He wanted to protect her, and himself, but wondered if he could.

"I made some calls," Pepper went on. "I knew he was originally from these parts. I'm sure, subconsciously, that was why I first moved up here. He's living in a little town just north of Rangeley."

"I know."

"You know?"

"I made some calls myself. Or rather, some visits." He explained how he'd located the man in hopes of finding a clue to Pepper's whereabouts. "I knew it was a long shot, but I was so desperate, I'd have tried anything."

"Did you see him?" she asked cautiously.

"No. He was out of town when I got there."

"Oh." She sounded disappointed. "He's involved in the management of the Saddleback ski resort. I guess he's done well in real estate."

John could hear the hurt in her voice, knew she was thinking that her father had done all right without his wife and daughter. "I, uh, did speak with him when he got back, though."

"You did?" Her eyes brightened. "What was he...what did he say?"

John chose his words with care. "He didn't know where you were. He did want me to let him know if I heard anything."

"You didn't call him tonight."

"No. I felt that was . . . your job."

Pepper rolled over on her back and stared at the ceiling. "It is," she said softly. "I'm going to drive up there. He may not want to see me, but I've got to give it a try."

Turning on his side, John propped himself on an elbow. "Why, Pepper? Why now?" He had to hear her say it.

"Just to see him—to see what he looks like now, where he lives."

"That can't be all."

She looked down, took his free hand and wove her fingers through his. "I want to know why he did it. I've imagined all kinds of things over the years, but I want to know the truth. I was so young when it happened. I didn't know to ask then. By the time I was old enough, my mother was unreachable."

"Pepper?" She looked up, surprised by the fear she read in John's eyes. "What if you don't like what he says?"

"Then . . . I guess I won't like it."

"Will it affect us? If it will, I don't think I want you to go. I don't think I can bear anything coming between us—"

Shaking her head, she drew his hand to her mouth and kissed his knuckles. "No, John, it won't affect us."

"How can you be sure?"

"Two things, both of which I spent hours and hours thinking about while I was up in Newport. The first was your mother."

"My mother?"

"Uh-huh. I kept thinking about her accident and all. It was obvious, having watched the rest of your family that weekend, that you're an active lot. It must have been sheer hell for her to have been confined to a wheelchair that way for so long. Yet she wasn't bitter. She'd obviously come to terms with it...and moved on. That's what I have to do, John. I realized that I was letting what happened to me way back then paralyze me now, and I've got far less to cope with than your mother had."

Touched, John leaned forward to kiss the tip of her nose. "And the second thing?"

She eyed him more somberly. "I realized that I was doing the very same thing to myself—and you—that my parents had done to me all those years ago. It was like there was this self-fulfilling prophesy and I was giving it a hand. In my determination never to be hurt again, I was hurting myself. I don't want to do that, John."

He moved over her then, taking her face very gently in his hands. "You won't, sweetheart. Not as long as we can talk things out, not as long as we can always communicate with each other. If something's bothering you, you have to tell me. No more running from problems. Understood?"

She had only time to nod before he kissed her, and then there was only time for the reaffirmation of their love in its most basic, most timeless form.

VERY RELUCTANTLY, John went to school the following morning. Pepper assured him that she had plenty to do between her apartment and his house. But as it turned out, she got little done. She spent most of the day on the front steps talking with one or another of the neighbors as they walked down to welcome her home.

"It's so good to see you, child," Mrs. Burns said, giving her a warm hug. "Are y'back to stay?"

"Yes, Mrs. Burns," Pepper said, grinning, "I'm back to stay."

"It was crazy running off that way," Sally scolded a few minutes later. "You wouldn't have believed John. I mean, we were all worried, but he was positively beside himself."

"I know. It was stupid of me. But maybe I needed to do it, if for no other reason than to put things into perspective."

"What's to put into perspective when a man loves you that way! You love him, too, don't you?"

"Oh, yes."

From Sally's hip, Chrissie let out a well-timed squeal of delight.

Old Sam was his usual crusty self. "John Smith's a good man. He'll keep y'in line. That's the problem with women nowadays. Too independent for their own good." He batted at a mosquito and cursed under his breath. Then he dragged a huge zucchini from his back pocket. "Saved this for ya. Y'missed the best of the crop, though. Now, don't go cookin' it to mush and drownin' it in some spicy sauce. Keep it simple. Taste comes through best that way."

"Thank you, Sam," she said, touched. "I'll do that."

"And you watch out for those sisters. They'll bore y'ta tears."

The Thompsons didn't bore her to tears. They were positively adorable, inching their way up the drive with just enough of a roll in their steps to suggest that they'd just come from their rockers.

"There she is, sister," Miss Millie began. "It looks like she did come back."

"Ob-vi-ously," Miss Sylvie replied. "Welcome back, Pepper. We did miss you.... Did you lose weight?"

Pepper opened her mouth to answer, when Miss Millie spoke for her. "Just a little. She'll put it back on in no time, now that she's where she belongs. Her cheeks are nice and pink. You are feeling well, aren't you, Pepper?"

Again Pepper opened her mouth; this time Miss Sylvie supplied her answer. "Of course she's feeling well. Knowing how much her man missed her has to put a blush on any girl's cheeks. But it's not the same without you delivering the mail, Pepper. You added a spark to the town."

"And she'll continue to do so, sister, whether she's delivering the mail or not."

Mrs. Biddle, bless her soul, had more to say on the matter of the postal service. "It was so nice when you were here, dear. You were so punctual." It appeared that, though the new carrier was a pleasant enough woman, she tended to stop for coffee and donuts wherever and whenever they were offered.

Pepper called Pam, who, though she couldn't leave the library, was thrilled to hear from her and had only the highest of praise for John. Jenna, who promptly closed up shop and raced over to the house, echoed the sentiment.

"You're a lucky woman, Pepper. John loves you very much. I'm glad you decided not to throw it away."

"I am, too, though I did have a few doubts when he showed up in Newport looking like he wanted to kill me. But it was really lonely there. I mean, everyone was nice enough, but I guess I'd become hopelessly attached to you all." She gave Jenna a hug. "You've become family. Any objections?"

"No, ma'am. I'll take you over the stiffs at Hilton Head any day."

"You went? Oh, Jenna, tell me about it!"

"It wasn't really all that bad. You were right. Knowing I was successful myself helped. But if you'd been with me, it would have been much better."

This time when Pepper thought of visiting with Jenna's family, she felt no pain. Her future with John sealed—and with his family and the family they would have of their own one day—she felt unbelievably strong.

When John came home, Pepper regaled him with talk of her visitors. They were on the screened porch, snugly sharing the lounge chair, enjoying the waning warmth of the September afternoon. It occurred to Pepper that there was something nice about being there waiting when he returned.

"I'd intended to go over to my apartment to pick up some things, but I haven't had a chance to budge." She smiled. "It's been nice. They're such wonderful people.

I knew there was something special about this place, even before I met you."

John arched his brows. "Oh?"

Her eyes were bright. "Mmm. The people are warm and caring. From the start they made me feel like this was truly home. Even if you'd never come, I think I would have stayed around for a while."

"Without admitting why, of course," he teased.

"Of course."

He kissed her lightly on the forehead, then tucked her more tightly in his arms. "Do you still want to go?"

"Tomorrow? Yes. Do you think he'll be there?"

"The only way to be sure is to call first—"

"No. No, I think I'd rather take my chances."

"You're worried he might tell you not to come."

"There's always that possibility."

John knew, indeed, how much of a possibility it was. "You'll be disappointed if you drive all the way there and find him away."

"I'd still get to see where he lives. No, the only thing that really bothers me is dragging you all the way up there."

"I don't mind, sweetheart. You know that."

"I could drive up myself—"

"No way."

She slanted him a glance that was only half-teasing. "You don't trust me. You're worried I might keep on going."

His response was soft and gentle. "I trust you. I know you'll be back. I just don't want you to be alone. Whatever happens, we're in this together."

THEY GOT AN EARLY START in the morning. Pepper hadn't slept well, and she kept chewing on her thumbnail.

"Much more and you'll hit skin," John chided, gently snatching her hand and pressing it to his thigh.

"I'm nervous."

"That's natural." He was himself, but for different reasons. "You haven't seen the man in twenty years."

They drove in a silence broken only by occasional comments on the passing scenery. "Do you remember any of it?" John asked when at last they approached Rangeley.

"Only what I've seen driving around this past year."

"You drove around up here?"

"Not specifically in Rangeley. But there was many a Sunday I'd just get in my car and go," she admitted. "I'd ask myself if I remembered anything, but the only things that were familiar were the same kinds of things I noticed in Naples. Country smells. A general sense of peace. I used to pass through little towns and wonder— is he here? I never had the courage—or the incentive— to ask around."

They entered Stratton and John drove directly to the private road that led to the condominium complex he'd visited several weeks before.

"Is this it?" Pepper asked tensely.

"Uh-huh. There. See the buildings?"

"Which is his?"

"Let's park. It's over to the left. Number 304."

When he pulled the Scout into a space, Pepper tightened her fingers around his. "John, maybe we shouldn't. Maybe this is a mistake. I mean, if he wanted to see me, he'd have done something about it long before now."

"It took you twenty years. He's that much older—"

"And should know better."

"But he's set in his ways." John's voice gentled. "You've come so far, sweetheart. Psychologically. Emotionally. I know you; if we don't go up there now, you'll be forever wondering. I don't want that. I want our marriage to be free of ghosts."

Pepper saw the absolute sincerity in his eyes. And she knew he was right. "So do I," she whispered, then leaned forward to kiss him once. "That's for luck." She slid to her side of the car. "I'll be back."

By the time she reached the walk heading toward number 304, though, John was at her side. She gave him a grateful half smile, then bit her lower lip and walked on. Her eyes were filled with worry. Her hand trembled when it touched the doorbell.

As they stood waiting, every doubt she'd had pressed in on her. Brief images flickered through her mind—of the tall, smiling man who'd always doted on her, of the pony rides on his knee, the good-night stories, then of abrupt and uncomprehending loneliness. She shivered with the memory of years and years of hurt, of anger, of wondering. Sensing her inner turmoil, John gave her a gentle, supportive squeeze. With the reminder that he was there by her side, that he'd always be by her side, regardless of the outcome of this long-overdue reunion, she inched her chin up.

The doorknob clicked. The door began to open. Pepper's heart thundered in apprehension, excitement, fear. Then, raising her eyes the fraction of an inch it took, she looked at the not-so-tall, slightly balding but quite distinguished-looking man who was her father.

10

Smiling pleasantly, Andrew MacNeil looked first at Pepper, then John. He was about to speak when his gaze, of its own accord, was drawn back to Pepper, where it stayed. His eyes widened a fraction. His smile faded. His complexion—rosy, moments before—paled considerably. He dragged his teeth over his lower lip, never once looking away. It was as though he knew but was afraid to speak for fear he'd be wrong.

In that, Pepper had the advantage. She forced a tentative smile. "I remember your being taller," she said in a shaky voice. "I was so little. I had to look way up to see you."

When her father continued to search her features in stunned silence, John extended his hand. "Mr. MacNeil, I'm John Smith. We talked on the phone?"

Andrew swallowed hard and forced himself to look at John, meeting his handshake but quickly dragging his gaze back to Pepper.

"Hello, Daddy," she ventured in a whisper.

Only when he saw the tears that sparkled on her lids did Andrew MacNeil finally speak. "Pepper." It was a throaty acknowledgment.

John breathed an inner sigh of relief but remained in the background.

"I, uh," Pepper began, "I just wanted to see you—"

"Andrew?" A female voice came from inside. "Who's there?" Seconds later, an attractive woman not that many years older than Pepper appeared, slipping an arm around Andrew's waist. She smiled broadly at Pepper and John. "Hello."

Andrew cleared his throat. "Uh, Cindy, this is John Smith. And Pepper. My daughter."

"Your...Pepper? Pepper!" Releasing Andrew, Cindy threw her arms around an unsuspecting Pepper, hugged her soundly, then stepped back. "I'm Cynthia Hendricks, and I'm so pleased to meet you! Both of you. But what are we standing here for? Come on in!" As she re-entered the small house, Andrew stepped aside to let them all pass. Not once did he take his eyes from Pepper, who, though feeling awkward, handled herself with remarkable poise.

They found themselves in a small living room, simply furnished but elegant in its way. It was open and modern, with little clutter. Cynthia gestured. "Please. Have a seat. How about a drink? Perhaps soda...something stronger?"

"Uh, we're probably disturbing you—" Pepper began, only to be interrupted by the woman whose role in her father's life was a mystery to her. She saw no wedding band, and the woman had introduced herself as Hendricks, not MacNeil. Was her father a swinger? Cynthia looked nearly twenty years younger than Andrew MacNeil, there was nothing either fast or particularly sexy about her. Rather, she seemed to fit the decor quite comfortably.

"You're not disturbing anything," Cynthia asserted firmly. She looked toward Andrew, who stood by the fireplace. "I'll go get something, honey. Coffee and cake?"

Still looking at Pepper, Andrew simply nodded. When Cynthia had left, he cleared his throat. "Were you the one who made calls about me last week?"

Pepper wasn't sure if she was in for a dressing down. Her father's expression was somber, his stance tense. She nodded, "I, uh, I needed to. I mean, I know it's been a long time, but I—" she looked down and made a conscious effort to relax her fingers "—it was something I had to do so that I could go on with my life." She looked up again in time to see her father nod once. Then, wishing desperately that he'd say something, but sensing that, for whatever his reasons, he would not unless prodded, she went on. Her eyes scanned the room. "You've got a beautiful place. Have you been here long?"

"Three years. We bought the first unit that was built."

"I was told you do management work at Saddleback. I . . . when I was little I never knew quite what you did."

He nodded again.

John wanted to shake him. He was aware of the effort Pepper was making, could feel it in every vibration that came from her. He wasn't sure if the man was made of stone or was simply stunned. He was about to interject something to ease the conversation, when Andrew cleared his throat again and spoke in a formal, gravel-edged voice.

"When I first returned to Maine, things were rough. I was a sales representative for a farming machine company and business wasn't great. It was all I could do to support Sean and myself. Then I got a lucky break—a tip from a client. I took a loan from the bank to invest money in a shopping center, which did well enough to earn me a solid profit. With that money I opened my own development company. Six years ago I had a heart attack, so I sold the company and went to work for the corporation that owns the ski resort. We've been growing. It's a very profitable concern."

"Heart attack?" Pepper found herself nearly panicking. Six years before, her father would have still been in his forties. That was a relatively young age to have a heart attack. What if she'd been too late? What if she'd made inquiries, only to find that her father had died years before?

Miraculously, Andrew was attuned to Pepper's concern. "It's all right," he said more gently. "I've been fine ever since. The doctors feel that if I watch myself I'll have many good years ahead of me."

It was Pepper's turn to nod. She felt John's hand on her back, soothing her for an instant before withdrawing. She took strength from his touch. "How...how is Sean?" She remembered her little brother vividly, though knew he'd look very different now from the tousle-haired four-year-old he'd been then. There were no pictures in the room; she'd already checked.

Andrew was faster to answer this time. "Sean's fine. He's married now, living in Boston. We were down visiting him several weeks ago. His wife just gave birth to their first child, a little girl." The light in his eyes brought a lump to Pepper's throat. She remembered that light; it had shone on her many a time when she'd been a child. She'd always assumed it to be the light of love, but if that had been so, *why had he left?*

"Here we are." Cynthia was back, bearing a loaded tray. She set it down on the round glass coffee table, which was in front of the sofa on which John and Pepper sat. She began to pour coffee into stylish glass cups. "Where are you living, Pepper?"

"I...we're living in Naples." She accepted the cup that was offered her, but when she found her hands trembling, she set it on the table. "John heads the guidance department at Lake Region High. I'd been the...I'd been working with the postal service up until a few weeks ago. I'm hoping to do some tutoring at the high school later on in the year."

"Tutoring?" Having handed steaming cups to John and Andrew, Cynthia was slicing a coffee cake. "What subject?"

"French. I majored in it at college."

"That's wonderful! Where did you go?"

"Vassar," Pepper said, then shot a shy glance at her father. He was listening closely. She imagined she saw a spark of pride pass through his eyes and felt a pleasure that startled her. She'd lived her life without benefit of his approval; it amazed her that she should bask in it now.

"I'm impressed," Cynthia said sincerely. "Vassar's quite a school. You've got to be bright to get in."

"I did well in high school," Pepper murmured softly, concentrating on raising the coffee cup to her mouth without spilling its contents.

"You must have," Cynthia returned. She took a breath and sat back in her chair. She looked at Andrew, then again at Pepper, then stood up again before she'd barely settled. "John, come. Let me show you the back patio. I think Andrew and Pepper could do with a little time alone."

John was in total agreement. Before rising, though, he sought Pepper's gaze. When she smiled, silently assuring him she was all right, he stood to follow Cynthia. For several moments the only thing breaking the silence was Cynthia's voice receding as she led John back through the hall and kitchen to the patio.

"You'll have to excuse Cindy," Andrew said softly. "She tends to take charge of things."

"She seems lovely."

"She is. We've been together for nearly five years. She's very good to me." He was studying the dark liquid in his cup, raking his teeth across his lower lip from time to time. Pepper watched him, devouring his features as she studied them. He seemed to be struggling. When he looked up at last, his face bore monumental pain. "I'm glad you've come, Pepper. You had the courage that I lacked."

"I'm not sure it was courage that brought me here," she answered gently, unable to muster an ounce of anger against this man who was so obviously suffering. "It was necessity. Had I not met John, or fallen in love with him, I probably would have gone on forever the way I was."

"What way was that?"

"Alone. Running. Leaving a place as soon as I felt I was getting too attached to it. With John it was different. I fell in love with him before I could leave, and when I tried to escape what I felt, it was a nightmare."

"He called me when he couldn't find you."

"I know."

"Are you back for good?"

"Yes. We're going to be married."

For the first time since he'd recognized Pepper on the front step, Andrew MacNeil's expression warmed. "I'm glad. He seems like a very fine man."

"He is. He's made me see many things. In fact," she said, then grimaced, "if it hadn't been for him, I think I would have turned the car around today when I was halfway here. I . . . I wasn't sure you'd want to see me."

Andrew took a deep breath and looked down again. "I can understand why you'd feel that way. I wasn't much of a father—"

"But you were! Well, for seven years, at least."

"Then I left." The words hung in the air.

"Why?" Pepper asked suddenly, unable to hold the question in. Her voice was laden with pain. "Why did you leave? I never knew. I've asked myself thousands of times, but I've never been able to find the answer."

Andrew eyed her warily. "Didn't your mother tell you?"

"She said nothing. When it first happened, she was so upset. She seemed to withdraw from me, too. I was afraid to ask anything for fear of making things worse. She was all I had left. I did everything I could to appease her. When I was older and finally dared to ask, she simply shook her head and looked away. She was never the same . . . after you left. If it hadn't been for the doctor's reports to the contrary, I would have sworn she died of a broken heart."

Listening, Andrew seemed to grow suddenly weary. He took a long, shuddering breath, then sank into the chair Cynthia had left moments before. "I'm so sorry that you had to go through all that."

"What's done is done," Pepper said quickly, then forced a softer tone. "Now I need to know the why of it all. I'm about to get married myself. I need to know what it was that broke up my own parents' marriage with such finality that they never saw each other again." It was only half the story; she also needed to know how a parent could separate so totally from one of his children, as both of her parents had done.

Anguished, Andrew stared unseeing at the window, took another deep breath, then faced Pepper. "In a word . . . pride. Stupid, stubborn pride. Your mother and I were both willful people. We loved hard. We also had distinctly different attitudes toward life. Unfortunately, we didn't learn that until it was too late." He paused. "In those days it wasn't the thing for a man and a woman to live together. When love hit us over the head, we believed that we had to get married."

He took a sip of his coffee, and Pepper noticed that his hand shook. It seemed a family trait in times of stress. She very carefully kept her own hands tucked in her lap.

"Your mother had dreams of a fine life in the city. She imagined a huge house, luxury cars, fancy clothes, lavish trips. I'd been raised in the country and thrived here. But I wanted her dreams to be mine as well. When I saw how unhappy she was after the first few years of our marriage, I took a job in New York. We lived in New Jersey—you know the house. I commuted every day, but I was miserable. Your mother and I began to argue, about little things at first, then larger ones. She had the driving ambition that I lacked and she pushed for all she was worth. As the years passed, I began to resist just as strongly. The only joys in my life were you and Sean. Everything else was an ordeal, including, increasingly, my relationship with your mother."

Pepper swallowed. "I never knew. You never let us see—"

"It was the least we could do, trying to shield you children from the hell we were living. Pretty sick, though, when you think of what we went on to do."

There was a moment's silence. "What happened to finally cause the split?"

"I decided to move back here." His eyes had a pleading look as he sought Pepper's understanding. "I was dying. I hated the job, hated the city, hated the people. I had high blood pressure even then. I knew your mother would resist the move, but I'd hoped that, if we could retrieve the love we seemed to have lost, she'd consider it a fair exchange." His voice dropped. "She wasn't even willing to give it a try. She was furious. She accused me of all kinds of terrible things. But I had a temper of my own and, having lived on the edge for too long, I let loose. I was young and as volatile as she. I gave her the house, the car, everything we had. It was my way of throwing in her face all that our marriage had meant. In my anger, I just wanted to be back here, free of her."

When his voice cracked, he stopped. Pepper was thinking the same thing he was. There was still the matter of the children, of rationalizing the abrupt and total division of mother and son, father and daughter.

"The only real pain I felt at the time was in leaving you," he confessed, having recomposed himself. "At first, your mother insisted on keeping both you and Sean. I couldn't bear that. My children were my heart. *I* wanted you both. She claimed she'd go to court for custody, and I knew she might win. I argued that if she went to court I'd demand half of every material thing we'd owned. I knew I was hitting home with the threat but I was so livid that I meant every word." He gritted his teeth. "I swear, I would have given her the bare minimum to live on—to raise you children on—if it meant that she'd suffer the way I was suffering."

Forcing himself to relax, he rubbed the back of his neck. When he spoke again, defeat underscored his every word. "That was when we decided to split you up. At the time, infuriated as we were at each other, it seemed the only solution. A daughter should be with her mother, a son with his father." He cleared his throat. "So Sean and I left."

It took Pepper a while to ingest what he'd said. There was something . . . cold-blooded about it. "You were right," she said, with a calm that belied her inner chill. "It was stupid. Didn't you—either of you—come to your senses later, when you'd cooled down?"

He shrugged but couldn't meet her gaze. "I don't know about your mother. I never talked with her after that. As for myself, yes, I suppose I did cool down. But then there was the matter of pride. Sean and I were living in the house my parents had left me. I was struggling to make ends meet." His voice rose. "I was damned if I'd go crawling to her for anything, *anything*."

He looked up and, as though he'd momentarily forgotten Pepper's presence, blinked. "I'm surprised that I still feel anger," he resumed more quietly. "I thought it had faded. We never did get divorced. I think that while I hated her for what she'd done, for what she'd made me do, there was a small part of me that continued to love her. In time I came to terms with living without her. I adapted to being a single parent. But then . . . there was always the hurt of wondering where you were, wondering *who* you were."

Pepper could restrain herself no longer. If the issue was pain, she was the expert. "You had to know when she died. Didn't you want to see me then?"

The look that came to Andrew's face was so kind, so gentle, so beseechful that Pepper nearly cried. "Oh, I wanted to see you, Pepper. All the time I wanted to see you. Before your mother died, pride stood in my way; I wasn't about to give in. After she died, well, when I finally got the news from her cousins, they wrote that she had named them as your legal guardians and that, as such, they saw no point in a reunion."

"But didn't you argue? Didn't you once go down there to try to see me?"

"No. No, Pepper. I didn't."

"Why not?" she cried, brimming with anger and confusion.

Andrew was no more at peace than she was. Sadness, at that moment, added ten years to his features. "I was afraid. The letter they sent was not kind. It said that you didn't want to see me, that you were finally adjusting after having suffered through your mother's illness with her. It said that my appearance would disturb you and hadn't I done enough already. I agonized for months and months. I tried to imagine how I might handle your displeasure at being forced into something you didn't want to do. I tried to imagine . . . well, I could go on and on. In the end, I was just afraid. Sean had adjusted; he didn't remember you all that well since he'd been so young when we'd left, and I suppose he took his cue from me, just as you had from your mother. I decided you would be better off with your mother's cousins. They claimed to have everything under control. They returned every check I ever sent. I assumed you were better off without me."

"I wasn't," Pepper avowed in a whisper as she averted her gaze. She felt a nascent anger toward those cousins who, while claiming to have everything under control, had denied her so much. But that was another issue entirely. "I never felt anger toward you. I never once said I didn't want to see you. There was just this . . . this awful hurt. After a while, I had to force it to the back of my mind, but it was always there. It wouldn't go away."

"I'm sorry," Andrew moaned hoarsely. Reaching out, he faltered, then hesitantly put his hand over hers and squeezed her fingers. "I'm so sorry, Pepper. You've got every right to hate me for what I did...and didn't...do."

It was the first time he'd touched her. Pepper felt the warmth of his fingers, yet was somehow unable to yield to it. There was an awesome tentativeness to their relationship; she was almost afraid to grasp its rebirth. Still, she couldn't deny the fact of her feelings. "How could I hate you? You're my father."

Andrew MacNeil smiled at her then, and she melted to tiny bits. It was the same, his smile. It had withstood twenty years.

JAYNE ANN KRENTZ

A two-part epic tale from one of today's most popular romance novelists!

Dreams
Parts One & Two

The warrior died at her feet, his blood running out of the cave entrance and mingling with the waterfall. With his last breath he cursed the woman— told her that her spirit would remain chained in the cave forever until a child was created and born there....

So goes the ancient legend of the Chained Lady and the curse that bound her throughout the ages—until destiny brought Diana Prentice and Colby Savager together under the influence of forces beyond their understanding. Suddenly they were both haunted by dreams that linked past and present, while their waking hours were filled with danger. Only when Colby, Diana's modern-day warrior, learned to love, could those dark forces be vanquished. Only then could Diana set the Chained Lady free....

WELCOME TO

The quintessential small town, where everyone knows everybody else!

Finally, books that capture the pleasure of tuning in to your favorite TV show!

GREAT READING...GREAT SAVINGS...AND A FABULOUS FREE GIFT!

Each book set in Tyler is a self-contained love story; together, the twelve novels stitch the fabric of the community. The covers honor the old American tradition of quilting; each cover depicts a patch of the large Tyler quilt.

With Tyler you can receive a fabulous gift, ABSOLUTELY FREE, by collecting proofs-of-purchase found in each Tyler book. And use our special Tyler coupons to save on your next TYLER book purchase.

Join your friends at Tyler for the seventh book, ARROWPOINT by Suzanne Ellison,
available in September.

Rumors fly about the death at the old lodge! What happens when Renata Meyer finds an ancient Indian sitting cross-legged on her lawn?

HARLEQUIN Temptation

Rebels & Rogues

Dash vowed to protect gorgeous Claren—at any cost!

The Knight in Shining Armor
by JoAnn Ross
Temptation #409, September

All men are not created equal. Some are rough around the edges. Tough-minded but tenderhearted. Incredibly sexy. The tempting fulfillment of every woman's fantasy.

When it's time to fight for what they believe in, to win that special woman, our Rebels and Rogues are heroes at heart. Twelve Rebels and Rogues, one each month in 1992, only from Harlequin Temptation. Don't miss the upcoming books by our fabulous authors, including Ruth Jean Dale, Janice Kaiser and Kelly Street.

HARLEQUIN SUPERROMANCE®

A PLACE IN HER HEART ...

Somewhere deep in the heart of every grown woman is the little girl
she used to be....

In September, October and November 1992, the world of childhood
and the world of love collide in six very special romance titles. Follow
these six special heroines as they discover the sometimes heart-
wrenching, always heartwarming joy of being a Big Sister.

Written by six of your favorite Superromance authors, these
compelling and emotionally satisfying romantic stories will earn a
place in your heart!